First Hand of the Night

A Collection of Early Stories

Liam R.W. Doyle

Tragic Sans
Press

ISBN-13: 978-0692470213
ISBN-10: 0692470212

Second Edition: March 2016

Cover design by Liam R.W. Doyle.
Scalzi/Wheaton "Madness" image by Jeff Zugale.

WWW.TRAGIC-SANS.COM

CONTENTS

INTRODUCTION

The stories in this collection were written during, and immediately after, my time earning a Master of Arts degree in English. They reflect a range of genre, style and tone that form a sampling of short fiction that I am pleased to have represent my early fiction. Even the sample chapter included at the end, from my novel *Singularity Deferred*, comes from that era, having served as part of my master's thesis. This collection is, in other words, a snapshot of a writer in a moment of time.

Of course, these aren't the earliest stories I've written. Like many writers, I have a huge personal slush pile of scribblings and noodling, verbal sketches and abandoned prose that, like most writers' early works, should never see the light of day. Only artists, it seems are allowed to show their sketches and practice runs. Perhaps that's for the best—for some reason, rough and incomplete visual efforts often still have a regard of being "art." Though rough or incomplete written work is always regarded as the embarrassing scribblings made before *real* work is written. Or, if you're lucky, it may get mistaken as a postmodern slap in the face of conventional and bourgeois form. But if you're a writer, and you're *exceptionally* lucky, your scribbles never get seen at all.

Fortunately, the stories you hold here are not scribbles. Nor are they even the earliest stories that are arguably worth a darn. These *are* stories that were written by the me that first proudly agreed that yes, he was a *real* writer, regardless of the fact he hadn't sold a great American novel yet. The me that was work-shopping, and collaborating, and finally submitting work after many years of hiding it away. In fact, a couple of the stories included here have seen light of day in other publications.

In any evening of card playing, you have to start with a first hand. That first deal of cards that some players feel set the tone for the rest of the night. Here is my starting hand. We can torture the metaphor and say it's the first hand the fates and muses have dealt to me, the creator; or, it's the first hand I have dealt to you, dear reader, in a run of other (yet to be) works and publications by my hand. Either way, it is a beginning that we have here, and beginnings are exciting and gripping moments!

A PRICE IN EVERY BOX

This story began life as a writing workshop assignment: "A girl sitting on a bench with a suitcase next to her. Now . . . write!" Naturally, first thoughts were the usual, "She's waiting on a bus to take her to a new life," or, "She's escaping a bad life" . . . but those were just too easy. What if she's not going anywhere? What if what was in the suitcase wasn't clothes? What if she was confused and uncertain about what was in the suitcase? *And after a couple of moments of mental doodling, a Pandora suffering from ennui came to mind and I wrote the story in one sitting. It was later published in* Moon City Review, 2009.

A suitcase was an embarrassing container for the evil of the world, but it was all Pandora had in her apartment to store him in. The wheels on the suitcase broke off when she got it nearly to the first landing of her apartment building. While they weren't a great help, the plastic rollers had, for a while, helped her round the top of each step.

She pulled and strained halfway to the second landing when Craig from 3C ascended into view and offered a hand. Craig was annoying, crude, and every afternoon when they passed in the foyer he would give his latest unasked for assessment of what was helping the country descend to hell in a hand basket. Fearing what she would have to gift him in increased attention in return for his assistance, she reluctantly dismissed his offer to help her—but he would have none of it. With a smile and a grunt, Craig grabbed hold the bottom of the suitcase and helped lift the container to Pandora's fourth floor landing. He gave her a wave and a "Have a good day," and flitted back down the staircase whistling a cheery tune. Craig: still annoying, though now *differently* annoying.

Craig was just the latest in a disturbing trend she noticed. An hour after evil's capture and already things all around her started to seem different. She realized she hadn't heard a car horn in quite some time, the constant buzz of people yelling at each other from open windows had transformed to the bleat of compliments and well-wishing, and the only time she heard a siren—it was followed by the laughter of children the cop had been entertaining.

She had been searching for evil, for *him*, how long now? So long she couldn't recall. In fact, there were years, centuries, in there she had even forgotten her search altogether. Nevertheless, she finally remembered earlier this year, after she dumped her latest boyfriend (and it was she who dumped him, don't let him tell you any different) when her existential angst led to her realize she had been asleep on the job.

It was a lucky break when she found him conveniently down the block from her apartment, across from the Fifth Street deli she ate much too many carbs in. And now it sat in a scuffed Samsonite, leaning against her apartment door. She didn't give much thought as to why he, it, evil personified was in the city, her own city, on the same block that she took her morning jogs down. But if there was anything "Uncle" Zeus had constantly scolded her on, it was her thoughtlessness. Now she would show him, she thought.

She got evil . . . him, it (she always did have problems with what to call it, him, her, since he liked to change shapes and genders at a whim—one of the reasons recapturing him after she released him from his golden cage had proven nearly impossible) across her threshold and unceremoniously

2

plunked the suitcase on its back in the hallway. She latched the three locks on her door, even though she realized it probably was no longer necessary. Pandora sat on the deep walnut-brown wood floor next to the suitcase. He hadn't made a sound all this time since Pandora accosted him on the street, which she found quite odd. No complaints, no bargaining, no threats. She knew he was the master of trickery and deception, so she couldn't quite understand why he put up no fight and didn't attempt to trick his way out of this.

Unless, his silence *was* a trick.

Pandora fingered the diminutive silver padlock that bound the zippers together. She should check, just to make sure he was in there. Maybe he'd escaped. Maybe, somehow, he had swapped something else in his place at the last second and she never realized. She imagined flinging open the suitcase to find a fire hydrant or a potted plant or a flood of endless joke springing snakes. She had to know . . . *had* to make sure. . . .

The matching diminutive key found its way home, she started to turn it, expecting the dry *chunk* of the lock popping open—when the ring of the telephone snapped her out of the trance. She pocketed the key with a glare at the luggage, blaming it for being inherently cruel to her overactive sense of curiosity, and padded to the telephone in the living room.

"Where is he?" the fierce and earnest voice on the other end immediately demanded.

"Who? What?" She was still somewhat addled from her earlier reverie.

"You know I know when he's contained; we're bonded."

"Skathi? How did you get my number?" Pandora was rattled: The women of the Norse pantheon always intimidated her. Her fellow Olympian immortals were generally haughty at best and passive-aggressive at worst. The Norse were just aggressive.

"Like I can't use Information?"

"But I'm not—"

"I called Nezha, alright?"

God, Pandora thought. *I go out with the guy for one decade and ever since he's still stalking me, keeping track of me—and everyone knows it.* She was equally bothered by the fact that Nezha only semi-stalked her, from afar. If he was forward about it, creeped around where she lived, she could have called in a favor and have him smote. As it was, he was just her long-distance snoop. *I have got to stop getting involved with tricksters!*

Speaking of which: Skathi reminded her, "Ever since that issue with Baldr, Loki and I have been psychically connected. I know when he's bound, and I know when he's roaming the world." Pandora actually felt sorry for Skathi, despite the goddess's ire. Skathi was also someone who tended to fall for the bad boys and get herself into trouble. She wasn't bonded to Loki just because of Baldr; she didn't *have* to be involved with Loki's punishment for killing Baldr. No, Odin had been pissed at her for breaking the heart of his daddy's-boy son, Heimdall (Heimmy to all those who liked to see him get all worked up and in a snit, which was daily) by dumping him in favor of Loki, who ended up breaking *her* heart in turn.

"Why do you think *I* have him?" Pandora asked. She held the phone to her face with both hands. "There's any number of deities and demi-gods who have it out for him. Loki's upset a lot of people over the millennia."

"Because you're the only one compelled to actually find him. You know everyone else has come to the agreement that, total jerk-wad bastard or not, the mortal world's better off with him free."

That kind of stung. It was true that since the day Pandora released Loki from the cage, and thus allowed him to infuse the planet with his evil and wickedness, she had been marked by the often embarrassing obsession to capture him. (Embarrassing because she was pitifully pathetic at the task of tracking him.) Granted, she had that period where the obsession was more of a nagging feeling that she'd forgotten something or had to be somewhere she couldn't recall and was ten minutes late—but even an immortal obsession can get kind of old after a few centuries.

"That can't be true. What about Odin? His precious Armageddon can't happen without Loki locked up."

Skathi sighed. "That's 'Ragnarök.' And you know the dirty one-eyed codger's been missing since Arbor Day, fifteen-sixty-three." Pandora recalled something about a disagreement regarding an old god-folk's home from which Odin was last seen ambling away as his kids threw spears and lightning and lightning-spears at each other. "Plus, unlike some god's End Day Party, Ragnarök's not actually a good time for the geezer."

"Well, I know Apollo would—"

"Don't mention that jerk's name around me!"

"What? Apollo may have moved on after I let Loki out, but I know he still cares about him."

"That narcissistic prig couldn't care about his own mother. Sister. Whatever! You know, you Hellans are a freakin' sex crazed incestuous lot. Makes me sick."

"Look, just because you and Loki had a thing and then he and Apollo hooked up, isn't Apollo's fault."

"He made Loki his bitch."

Pandora couldn't help it, "Skathi, Loki can change into whatever he wants."

"You know what I'm talking about! Masks and whips and cages. Disgraceful, to treat one of us that way."

"'One of us'?" She switched the phone to the other ear and ground a knuckle of her other hand into the end table. "Skathi, I have a feeling you're not talking about 'us' as in 'us immortals.' I know for a fact some of you frosties are into the alternative lifestyles. Take Foresti: I'd heard he's not all straight and narrow as he puts on."

"You leave him out of this!"

"This is a racial thing, isn't it? You can't stand the idea that your precious Loki, whom you've never gotten over, would dare be in a relationship with one of *our* dirty lot. You know, you're a real piece of work, ice princess. Maybe I do have Loki. Maybe I have him stuffed in a suitcase. Maybe he's shoved in there with a forgotten penny, a travel toothbrush, a sock, and you know what? Maybe he *likes* it. What do you think about that, ice princess?"

"You . . . you. . . ." The dark, smoldering rage was palpable through the phone line—a quality ever so literal when the person on the other end was a god.

Pandora's flare of bravery and gumption fizzled. "Leave me alone," she said in a cracking voice and disconnected the call. She looked across the room and down the hall at the bag sitting motionless, forlorn.

"I have a feeling this is only just beginning, suitcase."

* * * *

There were no more calls that day, but early the next morning they started to pour in. Congratulations from the likes of Themis and Brahma (she *thought* Brahma was congratulating her—he tended to be incomprehensible at times, simultaneously mumbling and shouting and holding conversations with himself), death threats from Heyoka and Veles, and calls of concern and pity from Mariana and Artemis.

Pandora always admired Artemis, but felt like the quiet geeky kid sitting at the nerd's lunch table wishing she could sit with Artemis at the table for radiantly talented and popular kids. (Pandora thought the metaphors television provided for emotional angst were the greatest benefit of the invention.) Artemis was never mean to Pandora, and in fact, was always kind and sisterly to her—whenever she noticed Pandora's presence. She was the first to pat Pandora on the shoulder and let her know it was all going to be OK while the others in Apollo's circle of friends and family (that still hung around him) scorned and berated Pandora for making Apollo alternately weep and rail for a week. Everyone suffered while Apollo suffered. Pandora often asked herself "What would Artemis do?" when she was on the hunt for Loki.

Even Yahweh, who tended to petulantly ignore all the other immortals, called her up on the morning of the third day. Although, Pandora couldn't figure out what the purpose of his call was. At one point, she wondered if his call was even related to Loki's situation and the resulting peace and happiness throughout the world. After a while of suffering through the babbling and soliloquies, Pandora hung up. He called back immediately. She saw the caller ID display "God of Gods." She let the machine pick it up. He hung up and called back and this time the caller ID scrolled "Not Me, the I Am. Seriously. Pick up." Pandora rolled her eyes and went to finish making breakfast in her over-sized flannel PJ's and slippers made to look like baby seals.

The suitcase containing Loki remained in the hall all this time. At first, she spent hours watching it, sitting cross-legged on the hardwood floor. Then, on a pillow on the hardwood floor. A couple of times she put her ear to the black ballistic-nylon exterior of the suitcase and thought she could hear breathing, but was never certain. She finally had to throw the key to the suitcase's lock out the window. After a lady who had seen it hit the street returned it to her, after having knocked on the door of every apartment on her side of the building, Pandora flushed it down the toilet.

The confusion she had about why "evil" was locked up as Loki was locked up, while some of the other baddies were still around, nagged at her for a while. However, she decided the whole what-god-was-responsible-for-what-thing was more complex than she was able to understand. Besides, last she heard, Set was killed some centuries back and Satan always was just a big misunderstanding. Most of the other so-called gods-of-evil (as mortals understood them), weren't. Not entirely. For example, Dis Pater was pretty good at farming and Hades was, after all, just a bureaucrat in charge of dead people. As Pandora remembered him, he was kind of a mousy guy with a nervous tick. His most evil trait was that horrible comb-over hair.

Eventually, she went on with her daily routine. She would throw a glance at the suitcase as she walked from kitchen to living room with her bowl of cereal for dinner. Or she'd lean her head back on the couch and crane around the corner and see if the suitcase had changed while she watched her favorite television programs: mysteries and the kind of "reality TV" that claimed to show the hidden true lives of ordinary people (a truly guilty pleasure).

Finally, she realized she would have to do something about the situation: television just wasn't the same anymore. Several of the cable networks disappeared; the news channels that remained only portrayed touching stories of heroism and generosity; commercials (both the clever and the banal) that sold stuff, went away; and reality shows that weren't pulled with an announcement from network management that they were "just too exploitative of people," became tediously boring. This had to stop.

When her distant friend, Eris, called her, Pandora took the opportunity to ask her out to lunch. Eris sounded as though she had expected the request: "Of course, dear. I figured you could use some advice." They met at Dozio's and took a table alfresco.

"Eris, I just don't know what to do. I mean, it's been my goal, my job, to find him, for . . . gods, forever. And now that I have, I don't feel the least bit relieved or like I accomplished anything. I feel like, like I can actually feel the weight of the suitcase in my hall weighing on *me*. Even here, away from there, I feel it. It doesn't feel right."

"Hon, it's because it's *not* right." Eris sat across from her, stirring a cloud of actual sugar in her iced tea—not one of those unnaturally soft powders from a pastel-colored paper envelope. Eris wore a stylish and expensive, but quite conservative and plain, outfit and equally expensive and understated sunglasses. Her blond hair glowed in the sunlight more than it naturally should have, and made Pandora feel out of place with her t-shirt and cardigan sweater and dark hair pulled back in its usual ponytail.

As long as they had known each other, Eris enjoyed a certain ability to radiate beyond her radiant attire, while Pandora couldn't seem do anything but be plain and unnoticed. Despite the differences, the two of them were friends ever since Pandora's first birthday (which, unlike humans, Pandora got to attend fully grown) when Eris pulled Pandora away from the throng of chiton wearing fuddy-duddies and psychopaths, and taught her the art of slingshotting grapes across a room, unseen by your victim.

"How do *you* mean it's not right?" Pandora picked at the spinach and artichoke dip with a triangle of pita bread while Eris took tiny and thoroughly enjoyed bites of apple crumble.

"Look around. The problem with your daily shows is just a symptom of the problem." This was sounding familiar to Pandora. "Look at this place." Pandora scanned around at the faux Spanish décor and happy, babbling people around them. "Have you noticed anyone receiving a bill for their meals? Anyone paying their bill?"

"Hmm, no, I guess not. But I haven't been looking, really. There's a lot of tips on the tables, though."

"You haven't been out much the last few days, have you, dear?"

"Well, not really."

"Money is worthless. No one charges anything; no one is paying anything. The entire world's economy is running right now, as we speak, via gratis and barter."

"What about the huge tips?"

"A gesture only. Finally it's a sincere and non-compulsory gesture, tipping. But *only* a gesture as that paper is no good as legal tender. Goodness, even legality, laws, are irrelevant anymore. No one is breaking any, since no one even wants to."

Pandora smiled coquettishly, "I thought it was the *love* of money that was the root of evil."

"Bollocks." Eris examined a piece of shimmering apple on the end of her fork. "This is really good. Are you sure you don't want a bite?" Pandora shook her head. Eris shrugged and continued after relishing her bite of mid-day desert: "Panda, dear, what is money itself but a symbol of the distribution of wealth. What is wealth? The abstraction which separates the humans between the 'haves' and the 'have-nots.' Upper class, middle class, working class. Even the lower class have more wealth than entire villages in countries previously unknown to most of these mortals. When you locked up evil, you eradicated the concept of wealth and who has it. Did you know that, right now, with the mental barrier of money out of the way, more people and food and supplies are flooding into those disease-and-hunger infested areas of the world? Without money to limit people, make them feel like goodness and charity are only possible within the confines of a set and defined dollar amount, people are free to be completely egalitarian, generous. Unfettered charity."

Pandora scowled into her ice tea, no sugar, no lemon . . . please no lemon (they always forget—although not this time). "I . . . correct me if I'm wrong, but isn't that a *good* thing? I mean, isn't this what they mean by 'heaven on Earth'?"

"Is it?"

Pandora chuckled, "Oh don't do that."

"Yes?"

"That whole answer a question with a question. When did you get your psychiatrist's license?"

Eris smiled and carefully blotted the corners of her mouth with the cloth napkin. "I'm serious, Panda, dear. Ask yourself, is it better or not?"

"Well, sounds like millions of more people living, thriving. I guess no wars, or crime."

"And no egotism, pride, desire, or ambition. Without war, chances are no sonar, GPS, the Internet. Velcro. Without ambition, no great American novels. No discovery of the South Pole or any humanity-inspiring acts of courage and bravery. Without desire: art, music, poetry would be significantly less inspirational and compelling."

"You can't be certain of any of that. You can't know any of that won't, wouldn't, be done without the bad side of humanity."

"Perhaps." Eris leaned back, hanging an arm over the back of the chair. "But do you want to take that chance?"

"Even if it doesn't, is that so bad for them? So they don't have a Mount Everest littered with discarded oxygen bottles and power-bar wrappers. They don't have the Mona Lisa. They'll have peace and. . . ."

"And over-population until pandemics wipe most of them out." Eris swung her arm back and hit the person behind her in the side.

The man turned around in his chair and smiled, "Oh, sorry."

"Eris," Pandora replied, "you're not seriously suggesting that the world needs wars as population control."

"Yes, but that's only a part of the need for humanity to have the whole their nature returned." She swung her arm back and smacked the man again. The man turned, smiled sincerely though a little confused, and apologized again. Eris continued, "Without ambition and desire they may just accept the nature of . . . nature, and continue providing aid and charity to each other while they wallow in death and misery, smiling all the while." She smacked the guy again. Again the guy turned, laughing as if he were a part of a grand joke, and apologized. "No eventual push into space, allowing this mortal race to survive the destruction of this cradle. No evolution of the species into an exciting and unimaginable posthuman unknown. Plus," Eris continued, "I like the Mona Lisa. She reminds me of you." She smacked the guy again. Now everyone at his table started laughing and play-smacking each other.

Pandora smiled at Eris, but felt sad and a little disgusted by the simple, innocent love-zombies at the next table. She had to lower her eyes. "So, what do I do?" she asked quietly.

"As I always say, dear, 'everything in moderation.'"

Pandora looked back up from under her eyebrows, "*When* do you *ever* say that?"

"Why, when it's to my advantage, of course." Eris popped the last bite of rich, golden apple crumble into her treacherously demure mouth.

* * * *

With the help of Eris' three-hundred pound bear-like driver, Package Loki was loaded into the trunk of the black sedan.

"I'm proud of you, Panda, dear," Eris told her as they stood on the sidewalk. The early evening air started to cool, and Pandora wrapped her sweater around herself. "I would have certainly expected you to have opened the suitcase by now. After all, it only took two hours for you to open his cage after being warned not to at Apollo's soirée." She looked wistfully at the gray sky. "Seems like eons ago."

Pandora playfully nudged her friend, "It *was* eons ago."

"And I don't look a day older, do I?" Eris chuckled at her own joke, told in some variation or another at every visit of hers. Pandora smiled.

Then she said, "You know, not to be ungrateful for your helping me out here, but somehow I get the feeling that you're taking him more for your own enjoyment than any real desire to help humanity."

Eris gasped. "Child, I'm insulted that you would suggest I would do anything purely for the sake of altruism! It's as if you didn't know me at all." Her driver, having gotten everything situated, stood, impassive and impressive, with his hands clasped in front of him, next to the rear passenger door. "It just so happens everyone gains in this situation, despite my better nature. Can I be blamed for unlucky accidents?" She playfully nudged Pandora back.

"So you'll let him out in short sessions?"

"Twice a day for one hour each, when he's good. Leashed, of course. I may hobble him and allow him to serve guests now and then. That should be good fun, especially when Golden Boy is among the guests. I can see his twisted self-righteous mug already."

"Hmm." Pandora looked down the street. No cars—only bicyclists and pedestrians. She wondered what evil in moderation will end up looking like. "I'm curious, though, why he never said anything."

"What's that, dear?"

"These last few days. No tricks, no conniving. It was almost like he walked into my life after centuries of being a myth to even me, and waited passively for whatever was to happen . . . happen."

Eris gently took Pandora's hands in her own. "Panda, dear, being a one-trick pony gets wearying even for us avatars."

"Yeah, I think I know what you mean."

Eris smiled at her friend. "Goodbye, dear. Promise you'll visit soon."

They kissed cheeks, and Pandora replied, "Promise. Be sure to take care of the little guy."

"Oh, honey, nobody's in better care than in Mistress Eris' hands."

The driver opened the sleek black door for her, and then went around to the driver's side. Pandora stood, ends of each sleeve bunched up in her fists, and watched as the car bolted from the curb, causing several pedestrians to jump out of the way and bicyclists to crash in comedic piles of limbs and spinning tires and shouted apologies. She waited to make sure there didn't appear to be any seriously injured innocent souls, and then went back into her apartment building, passing whistling Craig on his way out. She absently hoped the short sessions would be enough to inspire the return of her reality shows.

FOR WHOM THE TINKER TOILS

This is one of my favorite stories, and one of the hardest I've had to write. I struggled with every aspect of it: characterization, setting, story, even word choice half the time. Usually, which is the case with every other story in this collection and most I have ever written, a story will come to me and it just flows onto the page—rough, perhaps, and certainly in need of polish, but I rarely have to struggle to pull the story into the world as I had with this one. And yet, perhaps because of that, I have a certain affinity for this stubborn story that forced me to work for its existence, daring me to give up on it every moment. I didn't; I toiled on (and honestly, it is only now, writing this introduction years later, that I see the title this story selected for itself may be speaking about the author as well), and now have a story that I look at like a willful but dearly loved child.

The mechanized man with the blue markings swung the sword, that was as tall as he was, through the last two of the soldiers from the other side. The soldiers had nothing but their wool uniforms and were easily cut in half. Jon grimaced as he watched this, though at the distance he was he couldn't see much detail.

The other mechanized man, painted with yellow markings, punched the remaining soldier from the blue side, likely breaking his neck, then leveled his gun at the blue mechanized man. Even from far away, Jon could tell the gun was less a rifle and more a small cannon with a bore large enough for him to be able to stick his leg in.

The blue one brought his sword up, overhand and parallel with the ground, and thrust it down into the head of the yellow one just as his victim fired his hand cannon into the blue's chest. Jon heard the resulting boom nearly a second later and felt the concussion in his own chest. His mule, Toothy, reacted to the sound then quickly appeared as though nothing happened. The mechanized men stopped moving as one's head was destroyed by the blade easily as wide as Jon, and the other had a smoking hole through its middle.

Jon waited a moment, looking over the battlefield. He'd only just arrived, moments earlier, when he heard the sound of battle from the road and watched the last few humans and the two walking suits of armor slaughter each other. And now, there was nothing. No sound, no movement. Only bodies and trails of smoke here and there. At the far end of the open field were two giant metal boxes. Jon assumed they were flying carriers that brought these groups of soldiers to this previously uninteresting piece of land.

He wondered, briefly, who they were and why did they choose this place in all the world to have this fight. It was too late to get any answers and, truth be told, he didn't really much care. So long as the battle wasn't brought to his village, they could hold their wars wherever they wanted.

He picked his way across the field, occasionally stepping over and around bodies. He was glad no one was moving and there was no moaning or calling out. If he'd discovered anyone still alive, he wasn't sure he'd know what to do to help. He was a trader, a tinkerer, a metalsmith–not a physic, and the village and its doctor was a good hour away.

Jon reached the two metal men, locked in death. Yellow was pinned to the ground by the sword still clutched in blue's hands, who was stopped on top of yellow's gun. The metal around the edge of the hole in blue's back was ragged and curled. Now that he was next to them, it was easy to see the metal men were twice as big as he. He eased around the tableau and peeked into the hole in blue's back, and beyond a devastated layer of cables was the bloody and devastated torso of a human. The metal men were indeed suits of armor that completely enclosed the wearer. And, by the looks of the remains in the hole and the pieces that made up the suits' joints, the suit also moved from a different power than human muscle.

Who they belonged to, who these men inside were, also made only a pause in Jon's mind. Why only these two among the three or four score bodies didn't matter. Maybe they were royalty, maybe they were wealthy. All Jon knew was that they were now as dead as everyone one else in the field, and didn't have any more use for their suits.

He went back to the road and led Toothy, and the cart he pulled, through the field and up to the metal suits. It wasn't easy getting them loaded up onto the cart, but with makeshift ramps, rope, and Toothy's grudging help, Jon eventually rolled out onto the road with both suits. And, unfortunately, the men inside them. That fact was distasteful to him, but there wasn't anything to do for it until he got back home and figured out how to open the suits.

The cart creaked and groaned with the weight, and Toothy had to be frequently motivated, but Jon figured they should be able to get back to town before nightfall. Fortunately, he'd left Greenwood that morning just before sunrise, with an empty cart after dropping two plow blades.

About an hour down the road, as he approached the eastern crossroads, Jon had to drive the cart off to the edge of the road to make way for a column of men and a couple of large motorized trucks. The men were dressed in mismatched and ill-fitting pieces of uniform resembling one of the two sides back at the field–which was apparently where they were marching off to. They must have been coming from the city up north, which was a full day's walk to be sure. He wondered why they didn't get to use one of those flying carriers like were now sitting abandoned back at the field. Jon noted a variety of expressions as he looked down on the men of various ages, ranging from fear to barely contained excitement. Many carried rifles of various types, but most had spears and pikes, sickles and scythes, wheat flails and hunting bows.

But what interested him most were the three trucks. The rubber tires were nearly as tall as the cart, and the engines belched black smoke into the misty air. Jon had the opportunity to get a good look at a gas engine once, but it was so old and rusted he couldn't get any of the parts to move. Even so, he felt he understood well enough how it must work. But then, he'd always been good at figuring out how mechanical things worked. His father, five years dead this autumn, saw that and encouraged him to tear things up and put them back together all through his childhood. His grandfather, on the other hand, tolerated his presence only so long as Jon was able to bring money into the house.

The passing soldiers and what must have been their leaders (as they rode horses and wore complete uniforms) barely noticed Jon as they passed. One or two nodded at him, a few more scowled instead. Jon vaguely wondered if there was another column of similar men and trucks approaching the field from the other direction. Once the column passed, Jon made sure the tarp covering the metal suits was still securely tied, then continued on.

He reached his village just as the sun passed below the horizon and the sky had deepened to a rich blue marred with a swath of rust. Coming this direction, he had to ride through town on his way to his home on the edge of the woods on the other side. There were many people out at this time of the evening as people who worked out of doors stopped for the day, and those who worked in-doors would step out into the cool air and listen to the night insects start their music–before it got too dark and they'd have to put themselves back inside where the fire and dinner stew were.

He rode by Blackburn's store and Ham Blackburn himself sat on the porch smoking that stubby pipe of his. Ham smiled as Jon approached, showing teeth that were as crooked and discolored as the boards of his porch. "You got those barrels I asked ya for last week?" Puff puff.

"Inna couple days."

"Well, I'll be lookin' for ya." Puff puff.

Jon stared forward and drove on.

Halfway through the village, he rode by Bethany and her friend Alixa. They seemed not to notice him. "Bethany," Jon called. Alixa glanced up, then at her friend, then back down as they continued walking. "Bethany," he called again.

Bethany stopped and sighed, then turned to Jon. "Yes, Jon? What do you need?"

He slowed the mule (an easy task) in order to stay with the girls' pace. "Uhm, do you want to go to the river tomorrow?"

"No, Jon, I don't."

"Oh. Do you want to hike through Catchdown Trail?"

"We haven't done that since we were kids, Jon."

"Oh." He wondered why that should matter, but didn't ask.

"Can I walk you back home?"

Bethany stopped walking; Alixa stopped short. "Jon, why don't you get it? We're not children anymore; we live in different worlds now."

"We live in the same village."

"Different worlds, Jon. My father owns the mill and yours . . . you, do what you do."

"Yeah, OK." He looked down, and then back as Bethany with her hands on her hips.

"You still don't get it."

Jon shook his head. "Did I do something mean to you?"

She sighed. "No, you didn't. We just grew up. Now please, stop asking me to do things and go places with you. We're not friends anymore, Jon. Alright?"

Jon's neck and face grew hot as he turned forward in the seat and urged Toothy on, leaving the girls watching after him. He didn't talk to anyone else on the way home, including Missus Dell who called across the road to ask him if he'd stop to look at her new water pipes.

The road to his house turned off the main village road and quickly became a path. It was still muddy from all the rain earlier in the week, and, at one point, he was worried that the weight of the metal suits was going to get the cart stuck–but Toothy's determination won out. Finally, as the last of the light drained from the sky, the trees opened up and the house he shared with his grandfather revealed itself in all its patchwork glory. What started long ago as a cottage, over the years had turned into a pile of house parts stuck together and built onto itself. Generations of men and women who seemed to not consider tearing down and rebuilding was an option.

Around the clearing sat various sheds and shops and storage buildings. Jon drove the cart into the open side of the larger of the shops, the one he did most his metalwork in. He stoked the coke in the forge, lit a couple of lamps, then got to work unloading his cargo.

When the first suit fell off the ramp and crashed to the ground, Jon's grandfather stormed out of the house, lantern in hand, and called out, "Jon! Jon, izzat you? You know I can't see anymore like I used't. Is that you, Jon?"

"Yes, numpa. It's me."

"You just getting back? You're late! You're supposed to be back mid-day. I had to make my own supper."

"Sorry, numpa."

"You working on some new fool project? That Cooper got you making another metal fence he don't need?"

"No, numpa. Not for Mister Cooper."

"You keep making fool noises, keep me up, I'm not going to be able to net the creek tomorrow. My leg the way it is, prob'ly won't be able to anyway," he mumbled as he walked back into the house.

Jon continued to work on the suits through the night.

* * * *

The sun rose between two fir trees, shining directly on Jon's face as he lay on one of the workbenches. He sat up with a groan as a hot metal bar seemed to have replaced a neck muscle on one side. He rubbed and kneaded the muscle cramp while he stumbled blearily to the power suit that stood at the end of the shop. Most of it was covered in swaths of yellow paint, but there were pieces, particularly near the top of the torso, that were covered in blue. The remains of the suits that weren't needed to make one fully working suit were scattered around the ground.

The grisly remains of the men that were inside were wrapped in blankets in the back of the cart. Jon planned on hitching up Toothy later in the morning and burying the bodies in the family cemetery farther down the path. He had considered bringing the preacher up to the house to say prayers for them, as that was the proper way of dealing with the dead, but he didn't want to have to talk about them—it'd make him uncomfortable. And besides, their god would surely do whatever he wanted done with their souls regardless of what happened to their bodies.

Jon was glad for the sunlight so he could now see his work better. He spent most of the day working on the fine gears and cables, hoses and wires, that made the suits walk and move under their own power, guided by the person inside. It was fortunate, Jon considered, that outside the surface coating of paint, the two suits were nearly identical—it made creating one mostly whole suit so much easier.

He wondered how the two sides of a war would have such similar devices when it seemed there was only one to a side. Were they made by the same individual and sold to both sides? Were the sides of the battle once cooperative, and something drove them apart? This question occupied his thoughts for only a thin moment before it led him to think about himself and Bethany. Thinking about the way she chided him and sent him away made his face hot all over again. So, she seemed to wear her nice clothes all the time now instead of just on Prayer Day like she did when they were younger–that didn't have to mean they were suddenly different people, did it? Jon didn't feel any different than he used to be: He was the same as he'd always been, just taller.

Obviously, he decided, if she was the one who took it to mind to become a different person, that's not *his* fault, is it? She can be different if she wants; Jon was going to continue hopping the stones at the creek and feeding stale bread to the loons. Only, he'd just continue to do it alone.

Jon sighed as he wrapped a wire end to a tiny post in one of the mechanical hands in a way that just seemed to be the right way to do it.

Grandfather came out to complain about breakfast, then about the banging in the pipes from the well Jon fixed, again, only a few days ago. Then came out to complain about lunch, then about the tears in his net that have been there for months. Then, as the air began to grow colder and the birds called their tune to each other to find evening roosts, grandfather came out to complain about dinner, and Jon finally went inside to slice some cheese and salted pork and mix some garden greens.

"Numpa," he said as he stood in the dim house, "half the wheel is gone since I left yesterday morning. I don't need to make every meal for you," he said as patiently as he could.

"Boy, every time I pick up that knife I risk Mother's Luck in cutting my own hand off. You want me to cut my own hand off, boy?"

"No, numpa."

"I think you want me to cut my own hand off. Leaving me all day, out playing with your metal all day," he grumbled as he deftly cut his own serving of cheese into smaller bites. "Is that new bucket of scraps you got out there gonna bring in some coin, boy?"

Jon shrugged. "I dunno. Maybe." It occurred to him that all that day and the previous night, he'd only been thinking about getting a suit into working order, and nothing about what he was going to use it for. "It . . . will help me do work for people."

"Tell you what will help you do work, boy. Respect! Respect for your elders, that's what."

"Numpa, I . . . I don't know what . . . what's that mean?"

"See what I tell you? No respect. Darn fool boy, leaving his grandfather helpless at home to cut his own hand off."

Jon knew it was okay to stop listening, and he looked out the open front door of the house to where the growing shadows were cast over the nearly rebuilt suit of chipped and scuffed yellow and blue. He wondered if it would allow him to bend horseshoes into shape without hammer and anvil: He was supposed to run a new set out to Grayton's farm in the next day or two. That would be handy.

* * * *

The stars were brilliant and blanketed the entire sky by the time he'd driven the mule and cart down the trail to the family graves. Jon felt guilty that it took him a full day to remember to bring the bodies of the former suit owners out here. When he'd walked back out to his work shed after supper, he caught the smell he hadn't noticed in his concentration during the day. He apologized to the blanket-wrapped bodies as he hitched Toothy up.

He stopped the mule as the cart pulled alongside his father's stone, stark and alive in the swaying light from the lantern on the corner of the cart. Jon pulled out another lantern, lit it and adjusted the wick, and set it atop the headstone. The ground here was less rocky than it was nearly everywhere else, so it didn't take Jon long to dig a hole of reasonable depth next to where his father rested.

Since he'd began thinking about what the suit could do at supper, he couldn't help but wonder how long it would take to dig the hole if he used it instead of the shovel and his own muscles. But, he decided, this was the kind of work meant for hands and not machines. At least, that's what he imagined his father would tell him if we were there instead of in the ground.

He stood in the hole he dug, a good four or five feet deep–his head and shoulders just above the surface–and he realized his father was probably laying in the ground just next to his own ankles, over a few feet or so. Jon imagined the once impressive man floating in the ground next to him, as if in water. Reclined, peaceful, buoyed by the ground. When he stood atop the ground, his father below, the distance seemed as if they existed in two different worlds and not several feet. However, while he was below the surface, at the same level as him, it felt as if they were as close to each other as any time when his father had been alive.

Jon sat on the cold, damp ground at the bottom of his hole, the light from the lantern unable to reach him. He placed his hand against the wall of the fresh grave and felt the tickle of dirt shifting and falling from the touch of his palm. For the first time since his father died and was buried, Jon felt a desire to talk to him, as if now was the first time his father would have been able to hear him.

He had the desire, but not the words.

Finally, the sweat he had worked up earlier chilled him in the night air. The wind had changed sometime while he worked and Jon could smell the nearby sea clinging to the night. He stood and climbed out of the pit. Jon looked back down at his father's headstone. Once again, different worlds. He wondered why he suddenly thought of Bethany.

Once both damaged bodies were at the bottom, still covered in the blankets he decided he didn't really need so much anymore, Jon once again wondered about what the preacher would say about two bodies in one grave, and decided if the dead didn't complain, why should he think himself so important as to need to care overly much about it. He said a little prayer he sincerely hoped the preacher's god heard, and began filling the hole back up.

By the time he got back to the house and Toothy back in the barn, the Swan in the stars had moved across the sky to perch below the western trees. The eastern sky was just beginning to show a pall of blue over the black. Jon curled up next to the still warm furnace in his work area and watched the suit keep silent sentinel over him, until he drifted off into a deep and peaceful sleep.

* * * *

"Where do you put the coin you earn in that monstrosity?"

"You keep saying how you can't see, numpa."

"Even the dead can see that blasted thing you're walkin' around in like some . . . monstrosity, boy."

"In my pocket, of course. There's lots of room in here." Jon had just gotten home from delivering the Grayton horseshoes. When he woke up in the late morning, shaping new shoes was the first thing he tried in the suit. After he bent four beyond recovery, he finally got the hang of controlling the arms and hands and was able to cold-shoe two pair. The trip to Grayton's farm and back allowed him to get comfortable walking the suit.

He left the head off the suit so that his own could look out and about mostly unobstructed, but that hadn't stopped Tannor Grayton from taking a couple shots at him from across the field as he arrived. The bullets ricocheted harmlessly off the suit as Jon pulled his head down into the armored torso. The suit kept walking of its own accord with Jon yelling from within, "Mister Grayton, it's me! Jon Tinker, Mister Grayton!"

Finally, he heard a familiar voice shout, "Well stop that damn thing before it crashes into the house!" Stopping the suit once it got walking was trickier than he'd expected, but it was accomplished without any damage to Grayton's property.

"Well, did you get paid any more 'cause of using that monstrosity?" his grandfather was now asking.

"No, numpa. Same thing." In truth, he hadn't even considered changing what he asked for, for doing services for people, with the use of this new tool. Now that he had, it didn't seem fair that he would ask for any more.

As he walked the suit back to the work area, he caught sight of a couple of dark shapes moving through the air in a manner entirely unnatural. "What's that?"

His grandfather looked out over the trees to where Jon was looking, and said, "What'd I just tell you, boy? I can't seen nothing."

"They're boxes, in the sky." As soon as he said that, recognition came to him. They were flying carriers like what were on the battlefield two days before. "I wonder what they're doing here?"

"What? Where?"

They finally arrived over the clearing in the forest and the family buildings, and passed them over, before circling back around and coming to a rest within a blast of wind and sound next to the house. There were two of them: large black boxes, one with markings in white and blue, and the other with white and yellow. Doors and ramps appeared out of their sides and immediately several soldiers marched out, dressed in similar wool uniforms as their dead brethren had worn. Many of these soldiers looked as though they were survivors of the battle, but just barely.

Behind them, from each ship, came a man each dressed in uniforms with metallic decorations of gold and silver, indicating they were somehow more important than the soldiers. They were certainly cleaner and devoid of crusted blood stains. One of them, the one with a long mustache, marched directly toward Jon, yelling, "You, there. What do you mean by wearing the moto-armor of Lord Banyon?"

"You arrogant fool," the other, who sported a full, red beard, said. "He's wearing the moto-armor of Baron Lleweling. Come down from there and tell us where the Baron is or face immediate execution."

"Boy," Jon's grandfather said, "what fool mess did you get yourself into, now?"

Jon looked from grandfather to mustache to beard to soldiers and back to the puffed up and decorated men. "They didn't need them anymore."

Mustache said, "So you admit to the theft! You are under arrest."

"No," said beard, "he is *our* prisoner. Come out of there before we shoot!"

"The devil you say!" And the two decorated men continued to argue while the soldiers avoided watching it by watching Jon.

Jon decided it didn't matter one way or the other who was arresting him. He slowly turned the suit around and began walking away from the scene. His grandfather watched him go, saying, "Now, boy, don't go making it worse. You take your lumps." Jon kept the suit walking toward the road.

The soldiers must have finally gotten the leaders' attention as Jon heard two voices order, "Fire!" followed by the *ping* and *poing* of bullets hitting the back of the suit. Jon urged the suit to walk faster until it was running. At the speed it got up to, faster than he'd even gone on a horse before, guiding the suit became nearly impossible–which wasn't as much of a problem as Jon feared as it was able to crash through the brush and didn't give any impression of falling or tripping easily.

The sound of gunfire was drowned out by the workings of the suit once he started it running; though, by the time he made it to the outer town road, Jon was certain he wasn't being chased. He started urging the suit to slow down when he noticed a roar that overpowered the sound of the suit. He pulled himself up in the torso as far as he dared without the legs of the suit breaking his own inside them, and craned his head around. He could barely see over the metal torso, but he caught sight of the two carriers following behind him, occasionally clipping each other as they maneuvered for position. Whenever one did get in the right position, it fired a cannon that would blast a chunk of dirt, rock, and bush into the air.

Jon made the suit run as fast as it could, which caused the scenery to pass by in a blur while pieces of branches, twigs, and leaves flew up and around him. Until he ran beyond the sparse trees and out onto the plains where the obstacles became scrub and outcroppings of rock. He craned around again and saw that the ships had fallen behind.

Then, the suit clipped one of the juttings of rock erupting from the ground, and it completely lost balance. The gyros and servos, trying in vain to compensate, became a choir of mechanical screams of horror as the suit tumbled and rolled. Jon was protected from direct injury, but when the suit finally ground to a halt and lain prone, he took advantage of the pause while the suit's mechanisms recalibrated to crawl out of the device and scramble, dizzy and off-kilter, to a nearby cluster of rocks.

The suit, never given a new direction of action, righted itself and continued its mad run across the landscape, leaving Jon to watch after it, his back pressed against the rock while he breathed in deep gasps to alleviate the nausea. The roar of a ship crackled above him as a blocky shape tore across the sky in pursuit of the unmanned suit, followed close by the other nearly identical ship. Neither appeared to notice Jon was no longer in control of the suit as they never paused or deviated from following their quarry.

Jon continued to watch the suit as it became steadily smaller in the distance until, finally, it disappeared over the edge of the bluff and fell, still running, into the sea. The ships eventually stopped in the air above where the suit fell and circled in the sky for a long time before one, and then the other, of the ships broke off and flew back in the direction of town. Again, appearing to not notice Jon sitting, legs stretched out before him, against the rock.

Once he no longer could hear the grim and rumbling sound of the ships, Jon stood up, rubbed his weak and wobbly legs, and began the trek back home.

It was well into night by the time he made it back to his patchwork home. The ships weren't there. He grabbed the clay jug of water he kept out in his work area and chugged it, letting it splash over his face and run down his chest. Then, he went into the house.

Grandfather was asleep, snoring, in a chair at the table. A plate of cheese and bread sat in front of Jon's usual chair. The lamp's oil had burned nearly completely and left a struggling flame trying desperately to provide light. Jon put it out of its misery, and began urging grandfather out of the chair and into bed.

He woke up enough to growl, "'Bout time you got home, boy." A long pause, then, with eyes barely open and voice at nearly a whisper, "Worried." Jon got him down and pulled the musty blanket over his shoulders. As he stood up, his grandfather said, "Found bodies. Our graves. 'swrong with you, boy," followed by a snore.

Jon sighed, then turned and scooped up pieces of food from the plate left for him as he walked back out of the house into the cool night air.

The grave he made for the men that were the source of so much trouble, had been torn open—dirt tossed about in no sense of proper digging. *Perhaps they used something on the ship to just scoop the ground open*, he thought. Fortunately, the tear in the ground didn't reach over into father's grave. The buried men were gone, but what was left behind were the bodies of several soldiers scattered around the ground. Only on close inspection in direct lantern light could Jon tell that both sides were represented by the discarded dead, apparently shot by each other.

Jon shook his head at the scene. Nine or ten left behind to take two who had already been given a burial. *Well,* he thought, *the dead were dead regardless of their clothes.* Jon carefully pulled each soldier into the rough pit and, once again, the Swan had perched by the time he had finished shoveling dirt back into a single mound–darker than the dry and undisturbed ground around it.

* * * *

"**W**ell, I must say, that's the finest smoker I've laid eyes on. More than makes up for those barrels you took half of forever on. I'd say, that's going to earn you a fine consignment fee."

"Thank you, Mister Blackburn." Jon put the last of the ramp boards in the cart and tied up the rear gate.

"Say, you wouldn't happen to consider selling that arm contraption thing you got, would you?"

Jon regarded the mechanical arm that lay in the cart. He had made it from parts of the suits that the visitors left behind, and used it for all manner of tasks, including helping him make and move things like an iron meat smoker. "No, Mister Blackburn. Thanks just the same, but I'm gonna try hanging on to this one."

"Well, for the best, I suppose. Don't think anyone in this town but you could probably work that thing, anyway. It's as big as your mule and probably half as stubborn."

Jon smiled politely as he climbed back onto the cart's driving bench. "Nah, Toothy here's no problem at all. See you next week, Mister Blackburn." Without needing urging, Toothy started plodding forward.

Ham Blackburn watched the cart rattle and bounce down the town road and shook his head. "Odd boy, that one. Damn fine tinkerer, though."

DETUNED RADIO

Are zombie stories played out? Perhaps. Enough novels, television shows, movies have come out since I wrote this story that anything that comes out now has to be unique, creative, perhaps subversive in order to not be the subject of an eye roll. Is this story any of those things? I leave the judgment to you, dear reader. At this point, I'm simply hoping to entertain you if for a few minutes. Or at least make you liminally aware of a vague unease in your life. Either works for me.

John didn't know exactly when it was he'd become a zombie. Time seemed to slip by unnoticed a lot more these days. It had always had a sort of slippery quality, passing by his awareness with ease despite a rotund and heavy disposition. But now, since he'd changed, the days passed as a snowy gray blur. He had tried to pin down when he'd stopped being alive —it may have been last week sometime. He had a feeling it might have been longer. There was no particular moment, no significant event marking the change. It must have been a gradual process that started weeks or months ago, for all John could tell.

He sat at the breakfast table of his comfortable suburban house, spacious and child-free, while his wife, Julia, stood at the sink with her back to him. She kept the house immaculate. She seemed to have the extra time John felt was siphoning away. In addition to her hobby of keeping house, she was also an avid gardener and worked three days a week at a local florist. She had been generally unavailable for most of their marriage; she was even scarcer since John changed. He couldn't blame her, really—but it didn't make him feel any better. Although, he had stopped feeling much of anything some time ago. He sat staring at the empty plate in front of him, placed there every morning, originally from a sense of hope, then habit.

Julia rinsed out her coffee mug and placed it upside down on a washcloth. She left the room having said nothing all morning. John stared at the empty Pfaltzgraff plate in front of him until his watch beeped to tell him to go to work.

By mid-day John had accomplished a few tasks, filed a few files, typed a couple of reports. He didn't remember doing any of it. His productivity had noticeably decreased over the last few weeks, but he still managed to keep his supervisor off his back. At first Joe would come by his cubicle once in a while and ask him if everything was OK, if he was feeling well, if everything was fine at home. If he'd seen a doctor yet. Finally, he stopped coming around at all, except once a day he'd walk by and glance at John and walk quickly on, perhaps just seeing if that day was the day John stopped coming in. He felt like it would be acceptable, maybe even encouraged, for him to stop coming in to work. But he was compelled: Work had to get done.

He noticed he had been staring at the fabric wall of the cubicle. He looked down at the report he was working on and realized he couldn't make out his own writing. This filled him with a misty anxiety that swirled around his consciousness, creating thick and thin patches in his already foggy thoughts.

One thought stuck out in the mist and he lingered over it —there was another reason he found himself coming to work. Sarah. She worked in an alcove across the long, squat room filled with the maze of cubicles. He had always appreciated her presence, her flowing brown hair, her softly-angled face, the sweet smell of apples that seemed to float around her whenever she walked by or he had the good fortune to have reason to stand next to her by her desk, leaning down to look at something on her monitor. Her hair absorbed the falsely natural light from the fluorescents, somehow converted it to a brilliant and warm glow magnified and reflected back at him. Sarah.

His mind danced through these old and indelible thoughts more easily than anything else of late. They came to him effortlessly and stayed in his mind longer than thoughts of Julia, or his supervisor, or even how to spell the word "report."

John found Sarah, who was attractive and charming and compelling enough before, even more appealing now that she too had started to amble in a certain way. Her skin, still smooth and soft, had gradually lost some color. At first, John could tell she had tried to use makeup to cover her changing complexion. But sometime last week she stopped trying. Like John, she seemed to be going through the motions of the day, a musician playing an old tune—her muscles performing on their own while her thoughts were elsewhere. Sarah. Whom he shared something with, like an experience they alone participated in and had to keep secret, even from each other, as they went along their day pressing keys on keyboards, moving papers from one place to another, absently avoiding stumbling into people in the narrow walkways.

The day passed unnoticed until noon when the sound of bustling grew, and loud and laughing voices from various locations discussed lunch plans with each other. John grew excited. He almost felt his heart race. He put down the pen he'd been holding unnoticed, clenched, and opened his fist to work away the stiffness from gripping it for so long. Lunchtime was enjoyable now: not because of the pause from work, which used to excite him, but because for the last two days Sarah had come over to sit by him in the building's commissary.

Even after he found eating lunch increasingly unfulfilling, he continued to sit at his usual spot during lunchtime out of habit. For several days he still bought his regular sandwich, sliced apples, and diet soda, though he would end up throwing most, then eventually all, of the food away after sitting and staring at it for an hour. He vaguely sensed people beginning to appear uneasy with him around, but finally he was ignored altogether like furniture or one of the maintenance people he used to not notice. A couple of days ago, Sarah, who used to eat with another woman on their floor, (Becky, who had evidently found a new place to eat lunch and with new people), sat across from John without a word. She pulled out the chair and lowered herself with a slightly awkward grace John could still appreciate. She sat, staring at the plastic salt and pepper shakers, hands dangled at her sides, as if this was the place she was relegated to and had no choice in sitting.

She had sat in silence for several minutes, aimlessly looking around as if she was trying to find someone calling her name. John watched her for a while and finally said, "Uh, hi."

Sarah looked around to him. "Hi."

He couldn't think of anything else to say; the surprise of that unexpected encounter, after more than two years of admiring her from afar, relishing the brief moments of interaction they have over work-related issues, caught him off-guard. Finally, he said, "How're you doing?"

Sarah stared at him, then at the table, and finally said, "I hurt."

John nodded. They didn't say anything for the rest of the hour. The next day she came and sat down at his table again. They exchanged "Hi"s and nothing more for the day.

Now, thinking about the situation of that first day she had sat down with him, as if she had no choice, John's hands were on top of the table and he found them balled into fists. It felt like the emotion had finally caught up with him and he wasn't sure what he felt this eddy of anger at. Sarah? No. He felt sadness for her. She was more beautiful now, as he saw himself as more unattractive than before. She was a victim. She was being ostracized, as he was, and while that seemed like a natural progression for his own life, it was exceptionally unfair for *her*. Sarah, who generated light and apples from the air around her as an alchemist would create gold from lead. Her being rejected was a perversion of nature itself.

He looked around the room and saw everyone eating, talking, laughing, gesturing actively with hands and utensils, or staring at books or papers they may have brought with them. No one was looking at them; no one seemed to be intentionally *not* looking at them. They were being shunned as an afterthought.

This bothered him more than anything had for some days, causing his brow to furrow, a sensation which felt odd and foreign to him. John looked across the table at Sarah. The last few days she looked morose, sad, pained. Now she was impassive, statuesque.

He extended his arm out to her, palm up. After a few seconds her gaze moved to it, paused, and moved up his arm to John's face. She appeared to be thinking, her head cocked a little to the side. John nodded. Slowly, Sarah brought a hand up and placed it in his. She was cool to the touch, like a spring rain on a hot day. Their eyes met, he felt himself smile, very slightly. Her hand tightened around his.

They left work together. They didn't sneak out or avoid anyone—they simply left and John suspected the people they left were just as happy, if they even noticed, as he was beginning to feel. He had to concentrate on driving as the trip to the nearby hotel was new and outside his recently overdeveloped ability to act habitually. Sarah sat next to him, silent, but he felt she was as filled with a similar reawakened sense of nervousness and purposefulness as well.

He almost felt alive.

He couldn't tell if the woman behind the front desk

intentionally never looked up while she charged his credit card or she really was that interested in the small cube television on the desk. He didn't care. He almost chuckled at the thought of what she would think, two people in their condition stealing away for a quintessentially human act. The irony was not lost on his sluggish mind.

The room was small, had a single queen bed, cream-colored faux brick walls. They walked in and John stood for a moment, unsure of what to do next. Sarah sat down on the bed—it creaked and the thin comforter shifted with a sigh. Her gaze moved around the room, but she remained still. John walked up to her. His hand was surprisingly still and steady as he placed it on her shoulder. He felt the smoothness of her satin blouse like a single, clear voice singing through the roar of ocean waves. She looked up at him with a new expression. A plea, an appeal, something closely related to desire.

He cupped her cool face in his hand, the voice became a chorus. His muscles and sinew felt smoother than they had in weeks as he urged her back onto the bed. Each touch of her clothing, the skirt, the cotton underwear, was a new verse riding the crests of the sonorous ocean. As she touched him, slowly and deliberately, a look of concentration etching her face, John thought he could see the same sense of wonder.

The song ended some time later. An hour, two, John wasn't sure how long they were in there, but they had tried to continue too long past the point the sharp and vivid sensations had faded into the rest of the fog and they lay naked, still, on the bed for some time. At some point, Sarah sat up, stiffly, and pulled her clothes on in ritual manner. Before John had a chance to perform his own dressing ritual, Sarah had opened the door and walked into the harsh afternoon sunlight.

John dressed but remained sitting on the bed. He remembered the feeling of unfulfilled frustration he often experienced in his marriage—this was something similar, but seemed to encompass more than just his libido. For the first time he felt the dying process was complete; his life, his animus, was gone. Had it finally leaked away, or had they burned it out with their attempts at physical passion? He couldn't tell, but there seemed to be nothing left now.

He had to see Sarah again, one last time. It was a thought that, like most thoughts now, took up all the room in his mind leaving little space for anything else. John got up as quickly as he could and opened the hotel room door. He thought she left only a couple of minutes ago, she should still be visible—but she wasn't to be seen. The sky was noticeably darker than when she opened the door a moment ago. Time drained.

He saw the phone book at the bottom of the nightstand and looked for her entry. He found it under her husband's name, "Ellis, Kyle and S." John tore the page out of the book and left the darkening tomb of the hotel room.

It wasn't far, but the attempt once again to drive against his habitual course took every effort. As the day reached its gloaming, John pulled up to the well-manicured lawn of the Ellis'. Sarah was standing halfway up the walk to the front porch. John shuffled up to her. She stood straight, her head bowed forward causing her still messed-up hair to fall hiding her face. He moved in front of her. Her eyes were open, unfocused.

John's gaze lingered over her hair, tangled and dark brown in the gloom. He didn't know what he had intended to do. Tell her he was sorry? Ask her to go with him, away, somewhere to just disappear from the world that had already discarded them? Tell her goodbye? Moments after she walked out of the hotel he had thought of nothing but to see her again, and now that she was in front of him, stalled like a stopped watch in the middle of her lawn, he couldn't think of why he was there. But it felt right, appropriate, that they should be together.

It was dark now. It happened suddenly, like he blinked

and everything changed. The sky was black and the street lights were on. Sarah was no longer there. John turned around and saw the door to the house swing closed. Through the large window, he watched a young boy lead Sarah to sit on the living room couch. Her husband, Kyle, appeared in view. He was on a cell phone looking at John with disgust as he pulled the drapes closed with one hand. There was a car in the driveway that wasn't there before.

John stumbled away, back to his car. He felt what he thought was anger. Instead of the clear song over the waves the first tactile sensations earlier that afternoon produced, this was a low rumbling that merged and flowed with the ocean current that filled his head with foam and vortexes. He started the car and drove away, through the regular pools of street lights he couldn't see.

He blinked again. He was in a culvert. The car was tilted down, the engine still running but with a loud, repeating *chang*-ing sound. The depleted airbag cascaded from the steering wheel and the car was filled with a white powder and a smell he couldn't identify. He wasn't sure he could even smell it—he had a knowledge there was a strong smell but he simply couldn't sense it.

He shoved the door open and pulled himself up the embankment. He recognized where he was. He had driven most of the way home with no memory of it. He started walking.

John almost walked past his house. He didn't quite recognize it; it was a strange place to him, a building with no discernible purpose, gray and formless. He finally got the garage door open and plodded through the utility room and stood for a moment in the kitchen. The lights were off. The house was quiet and still. The clock on the microwave said something, but he no longer recognized the symbols. He remembered they were once a different color, but now they were a dim white.

He went into their living room, his and Julia's. Well, it had been mostly Julia's. John had always been more or less a lodger in the home. It took him a while to get up the stairs. His joints ached. He felt that. He felt an aching and constant pain throughout his body now, to match the ache that had replaced all thought. He vaguely remembered when the ache wasn't there. With Sarah. Was that earlier today?

The guest-room door was open. In the moonlight John could see the bed he had been sleeping on since Julia became uncomfortable with him. He walked past it to the bedroom he hadn't entered in days. Julia was a shape under the thick, down comforter. It moved gently, rhythmically in the silver light filtered through the diaphanous bedroom curtains.

John climbed onto the bed, hand over hand, knees creaking in the silence. He crawled on top of Julia as she slowly shifted and moved into semi-wakefulness. "Wha- John? What are you doing? Please, just go into the other room." Her voice was thick and slurred, her eyes were barely opened. She tried to pull the comforter back over her shoulders.

He pushed his fingers through her wavy pool of hair that would be blond in the light, and if he could still see color. The sensation was like touching white noise.

"John," her voice was edged with disgust. "Please. I need— "

He clenched her hair into his fist; she squealed in surprise, fully awake. John descended. His teeth ripped through Julia's cheek, through muscle, and scraped against her own teeth and jawbone as he bit with a force unfamiliar to him. She screamed, wet and sharp. Inhuman. She struggled under the bedding, trying desperately to get her arms out to protect herself, but his weight on the comforter trapped her underneath, unable to escape.

Her blood ran out of his mouth, hot and salty, down his chin. He tasted it. It was real. He bit again, tearing the flesh down to her throat.

He felt alive.

THE END OF THE BEGINNING

I'll be honest, I am surprised by the existence of this story. I'm not sure what prompted me to write it, I don't recall the writing process on it . . . one minute I was thinking about the heat death of the universe, and the next minute I was selling this story to M-BRANE SF *(#10, 2009). I am pretty sure I set out to write a straightforward sci-fi story, but then something happened along the way. Although, who says this isn't pure SF? Who are we to judge exactly what happens to the protagonist during the course of events?*

Ash was too late to see the end of the universe; it was already dead when he woke up.

At first, he had no idea what had happened. He'd expected to be floating in the secured testing area in high Martian orbit, or at least find himself surrounded (cosmically speaking) by the familiar planets and moons of his solar system. Instead, he seemed to be nowhere. Outside the viewports was complete blackness. The sensors picked up nothing nearby, then nothing at a distance, then nothing as far as they could scan. Not a single photon nor x-ray nor infrared wave nor alpha particle. Nothing.

He thought he must have still been asleep. The situation seemed too surreal, too hard to wrap his mind around, like trying to read a sign in a dream: no matter how hard one tries the words may change and shift or become meaningless. Ash tried to understand what the readings told him, but they made no sense. He would look out a port, see a part of the outside of his capsule in the dim illumination of one of his own exterior lights—but beyond that the dark was an oppressive, suffocating thing. His eyes kept trying to view through and past the impenetrable obscurity, into infinity, at something. The dark was absolute, unyielding and his eyes grew weary of working at focusing on the featureless black.

He considered the possibility that he was trapped in an alternate dimension. The entire process of time travel required the manipulation of at least two of the other seven dimensions humans could not directly perceive. A process barely understandable by those who discovered and developed the technology but made it work anyway. At least, they had made it work with countless unmanned probes. Ash was the first human to make the trip into the future. He was the "person of the bravest heart and noblest of will who would risk experiencing the greatest unknown yet to challenge the human race," so said the Prime Minister to the handful of scientists and technicians collected on the facility where the secret project was housed. No sense getting the hopes of the other twenty billion citizens of the doomed Republic up too early. After all, despite the fact that every one of the last several probes came back with convincing data proving its trip ten, one hundred, one thousand years into the future, the visual data was always blank with only vague hypotheses of quantum-uncertainty-this or Schrödinger-apprehension-flux-that, to explain it. It would require a human mind and adaptability to make sense of it.

It didn't make sense to Ash. He thought maybe this was why the probes came back with nothing to see—but at least they had telemetry data and sensor readings of being near the test theater above Mars. Readings of solar activity, debris density. Ash's readings, on the surface, came up zero for everything.

Then, after a couple days (according to the Martian Local

Time the capsule continued to calculate) of sleepless investigation and increasing body aches and illness, the answer became undeniable. Something had gone wrong, that was apparent from the beginning: He hadn't been sent one day into the future as had been planned; he had been sent hundreds of billions, trillions, perhaps googol years into the future—where all matter has decayed and there is nothing left in the universe except an ever-expanding fabric. This reality became apparent when the results of the dark matter analysis completed: The concentration of the invisible and normally imperceptible matter was a percent of what it should have been, which also explained why the failsafe return, should anything go wrong in transit, had failed. The dimension fold system was powered by the (previously) ever present and bountiful dark matter. But whenever he was, it was so far into the future that even the dark matter had either decayed or expanded so thin as to be, for all practical purposes, non-existent.

The moment Ash realized the unavoidable truth of the matter, he collapsed back in the only chair in his capsule. Part of his mind was relieved by the resolution of the mystery, the other was devastated by the realization that he was trapped. There was no possible way to return to his own time, his home (State provided of course), his daughter Lahya.

He dimmed the already faint cabin light all the way out and the console lights to as few and as low as he could, and stared out the main viewport. At one moment, he imagined the blackness was a cover over the glass, the next he imagined he could see the infinity of space. If he tried hard, he could see for an instant a field of stars hanging in the ink. But it was only fleeting phantasms. He thought about the fact that regardless of when he was, technically he was still at the same point in space he occupied countless epochs ago. Well, Ash mused, that's not exactly right. By this time, the eighty cubic meters or so of volume that his capsule once occupied was probably stretched tens of kilometers, at least, in all directions around him. He wondered if the expansion of space had indeed continued to accelerate, what its rate was now and whether it was affecting him in some way. The capsule was encased in a warping field that acted as both a shield and a lubricant, in a manner of speaking, for the dimension folding process. It was designed to stay up after the transfer in case any space-time anomalies are detected. The shielding was still up. Inside his barely stable pan-dimensional shield he was protected from whatever dynamic fabric-warping forces may be going on outside. In effect, inside his capsule was a fragment of space-time that, compared to what was outside, was as compressed as a diamond is to powdered graphite.

But the shield protecting him from being pulled into component atoms wouldn't last long—the small amount of contained antimatter fueling his capsule was being quickly consumed. Ash estimated he'd have at most a week before it and all other systems on the capsule failed. He didn't have to worry about food and water, however: Water recycling was an old and perfected technology, and emergency food paste took up little space and lasted for months. Although, the way he was feeling, food was the last thing on his mind.

Shortly after awakening from the cryo-sleep that was necessary for the folding—even though the trip lasts (to the human mind) but a minute—Ash began to feel unwell. And not the same kind of unwell that sometimes followed cryo-sleep and could be managed with the medicine he was supplied with. It started with the aches and all-over body soreness, like a flu. This should have been impossible as, per procedure, he had been quarantined for two weeks before departure and every millimeter of the capsule and all equipment had either been built or assembled in vacuum and sanitized. Then the stomach pains and headaches began around the time he discovered what his temporal situation was. After that, he had little motivation to leave the cryo bed where he would mainly lie in a fetal position drifting in and out of sleep.

What was the point, he thought. Sometimes as a fleeting question, others as an insistent nag like the drone of cicadas. If whatever was making him sick didn't kill him, the probable destruction of the ship in a few days would. And even if that didn't happen, food would eventually run out while he drifted in the void. People, ships and bases, Earth and Mars themselves, were probably eaten up by the galactic black hole before it too evaporated into nothing. Nothing was left. Nothing to do except wait.

His capsule contained a pistol. "You never know," the mission supervisor had said, "what you may encounter on the other side."

"I'm just going into tomorrow," Ash said.

"You never know when tomorrow may go wrong," the supervisor quipped.

The crude pistol rested in a form-fitting box clipped to the side of the console chair. He began to imagine what it would feel like to have ten grams of compressed carbon propelled on a cushion of magnetism rudely intrude upon the space in his head where his brain called home. Of course there were risks to his job. Every mission he flew for the State held a significant chance that he wouldn't return. It was something he never used to care about, when he would fly fighters in strike-and-fly runs while also studying theoretical physics at the government university. Nor did he give it much more thought once he was married. Many people died every day either fighting for the State or in daily terrorist attacks by the enemy. He, and his wife, and most people, simply expected to die early and violently in one way or another—it was just something you grew up accepting. And for that reason, most people held superficial and fleeting relationships with others. His marriage, unconventional as it was for being a one-man-one-woman relationship, was "normal" in that it was just this sort of relationship. He liked her well enough, but he just knew that one or the other of them was likely to not survive past forty; so, why get more emotionally invested than reasonable?

Then Lahya was born and things changed. It surprised him to discover previously dormant feelings of love and adoration, a desire to protect and nurture, and, oddly, hope. His daughter, that tiny, helpless creature with bright blue eyes, who would laugh wildly whenever Ash popped up from behind her, playfully yelling "Boogla Boogla!!"—his daughter gave him a sense of hope for humanity that he found unfamiliar, confusing, baffling. Birth rates were extremely high, cloning was legal and encouraged; there was actually more life being created than what was being taken away by ever-present war, rampant epidemics, flourishing murder and suicide. Yet the predominant mood of most people existed in the realm of despair, self-destructive patriotism or ideological fanaticism, or the default flatline feeling that came from a life of mere existence.

When he was picked to be the first human time traveler, once, Ash would normally have accepted just for the adventure. But now, he accepted because it meant hope. It meant humanity might have a chance to escape the tar pit of time and place it was trapped in. It meant Lahya might grow up to *want* to live past forty.

This mission wouldn't have required any real flying: the capsule only had guiding and emergency thrusters in case the capsule found itself in the way of something or caught in, presumably, Mars' gravity well. But that experience with quicker-than-thought reaction and decision making, along with his education in temporal and multi-dimension physics, made him an excellent candidate for being the first human to time travel.

"What greater endeavor can one person hope to embark upon than one in the service of humanity. To step into the unknown, to forge a path through the undiscovered country for others to follow behind—that is the pinnacle of bravery and a shining inspiration for others to draw courage from as we fight through these dark days." The words the Prime

Minister spoke at his departure ceremony were hallow and perfunctory to everyone listening—except to Ash. This was only a week after the previous Prime Minister was killed by a separatist attack.

On the end of the fourth day, trapped at the end of the universe, the pistol was floating listlessly a couple of inches in front of Ash's contemplating face, waiting to be used.

* * * *

It was sometime during the fifth day, when contemplation was turning to decision, when she appeared. Ash had been half awake, fading in and out, the pistol loose in his hand, when he saw movement in the corner of his vision. In a haze of pain and pain meds, he gingerly craned his neck up so he was looking at the console area of the capsule upside down. Nothing. There was movement at the edge of vision again. He eased his head back down and looked beside the bed. Nothing. *About time I started seeing things*, he thought. He drifted into unconsciousness for several hours.

Her voice woke him. It was singing: low and barely perceptible, but there. He couldn't tell how long he'd been aware of it, how long he had been coming out of the darkness —maybe a minute, maybe an hour. But he felt the singing had been there the entire time. When he opened his eyes, he could see nothing except a dim, soft haze with vague impressions of shape and color. When he tried to focus, it felt like his head was splitting open. If he did nothing, the pain was a background noise. He stared ahead at the formlessness, letting the singing wash through him. It didn't seem to matter if he could understand the words or not, or even if the music contained words—he couldn't tell. He just accepted it and let it happen.

In front of his unfocused eyes, a form separated itself from the blurred shadows and shapes and drifted closer to him. It was the source of the music, Ash was sure of it even though the sound didn't change. It seemed to be in his head. The form was human-shaped, and he innately understood it to be female despite its indistinctness. He felt it . . . her, touch his face. The contact felt distant and separate from himself, but he felt warmth. The warmth spread from his face through his body, and the ever-present pain lessened just enough so that instead of falling unconscious again, he fell asleep.

* * * *

"We commend Colonel Ash to the spirit of the universe," the Prime Minister intoned. Ash had shifted uncomfortably, unused to ceremonies in his honor. "May his search for answers be a revelation to us all." The dozens of hands of the assembled scientists and technicians clapped politely. Ash smiled obligingly.

* * * *

Ash woke up with the sound fading in his mind. He could focus both his mind and his vision a little better. The pistol had escaped his hand and floated across the capsule. That was alright, he thought. He could delay his self-determined exit a little longer. He eased himself up on one elbow and looked up and down the area. No one. He wondered for a moment how he could have believed so readily that there was someone with him in the capsule . . . last night? Yesterday? An hour ago? He realized he had no idea when it was.

Despite the weightlessness, it still hurt to move himself into a sitting position. He felt like one does after a fever breaks, like he was past some kind of wall; except, he could feel it was a temporary condition. It wasn't just a fear of it, he knew it was the case. Somehow he broke the surface of the sea of pain and delusion to breathe stinging, salty air—but he was still in the water and his head could dip below the surface at any time.

He looked over at the console. It was alive with needful warning lights. Ash unhooked the netting that hugged his body against the bed and pulled himself across the space to the chair. Sitting and then strapping himself in caused waves of pain to crest over his head, allowing him to stay afloat enough to gulp air in ragged breaths. He sat for several minutes trying to steady his breathing, calm his mind. He tried to imagine Lahya, asleep, watching her soft and steady breathing, which had always calmed him. At various instances when he felt his awareness dip into the fuzzy dark, he thought he could hear singing, but it would go away the instant he came back to his agonizing senses.

After he felt like he had some amount of control and not like he'd lapse back into his earlier incoherence, he scanned the console. Things were falling apart. Nearly every major system on the capsule was registering errors from minor, to threats of catastrophic collapse. The shielding was fading, the antimatter containment was on the verge of shutdown, half the sensors were indicating they couldn't communicate with various parts of the structure. The mind was losing cohesion.

Ash struggled with heavy arms to adjust various settings and processes to try to put as much power on the shielding as possible. He considered shutting it down altogether; it would be an easy thing to do. A quick override of the security and then a push of a button. He was certain the tissue thin, metaphorically speaking, fabric of space was at this point expanding so fast that his island of unimaginably ancient time-space would be disintegrated instantaneously the second his pan-dimensional shield failed. Even with the gun, he wasn't assured such a quick and certain death. Why wait any more? Why was he bothering to keep the ship and his own mass together a moment longer? Was it survival instinct so primal he had no control over it? His mind understood that no matter what he did, he could never see his daughter again, and hear her laugh and see her push herself with limitless determination up from the floor and crawl—but his heart couldn't understand it, not at this moment at least. Not long ago he was ready to eat the gun, but now he was willing to tread an ocean of pain that he knew contained no shore, only submersion once exhaustion overtook all—which it surely would.

He looked out the viewport. Soon he would be a part of that nothing. He had no real idea what it would look like, to a hypothetical observer. Perhaps if someone on the outside were to watch the point of space he occupied, they would currently see nothing as his own bubble of time-space was too compressed, too slow to be visible. Once his shielding failed, he might fade into view from a blue shift before having every atom of every molecule torn apart. He stared into the universe that at one time teemed with stars. At one time filled with planets of rocks and gas, and positively saturated with moons. So many, so abundant these other worlds, that there were many places that humanity could have moved to, most needing only minor changes. Dozens of potentially habitable planets and moons tantalizingly evident to the scientists and astronomers, but utterly out of reach. All they could do was see the evidence of a planet that could support life. To reach these planets would take thousands of years for a one-way trip . . . by then, each and every one of those previously Eden-like worlds could have dried up, or have been destroyed by a comet, or have had a sentient species evolve, rise up and develop civilization, and waste the biosphere with the same weaponry and toxins we destroyed our own worlds with. Dimension folding, time travel, these extremely new and barely understood developments could have been stage one in an answer to saving the crawling human race.

What did they do after I didn't arrive the next "day," Ash wondered. With so much at stake, there's no way they would have scrapped the project. They would have sent another probe, or several. Then eventually another brilliant, brave, talented, and ultimately expendable person. Perhaps they succeeded. Perhaps they went on to stage two, and three, and on to stage twenty, where they developed a way to slip ships through the Goridan Knot that was the higher dimensions and land them instantly in these new homes. It was possible, likely, in fact, that should humanity have found at least one or two habitable, stable new worlds to populate, it could survive to populate the galaxy. For all Ash knew, a million years after he left, humanity may have swarmed over the galaxy like feathery dandelion pods in the wind and even started seeding other galaxies. Maybe by the time stars were beginning to die without new ones being born, humanity had filled the universe in all directions until it wrapped around the infinitely finite fabric of space like a Mobius strip and met itself. Perhaps there were humans, or whatever humans would have evolved into by that time, trapped in artificial ships and bases and worlds, that were still alive tens of trillions of years later when the dark energy finally accelerated the universe to the point where molecules could no longer hold together. Maybe there were creatures, his race's descendants, beings who might have borne no resemblance whatsoever to being human, who met the same fate we would soon meet.

Ash no longer felt as empty and alone as he had before.

He wasn't sure he had seen it. At first, he thought it was a reflection on the glass. A patch of darkness a shade lighter than the absolute darkness. One instant it wasn't there and the next it seemed to just form out of the nothing. Ash looked into the cabin behind him, around him, nothing seemed to be making this shape he could, yet couldn't, see. He recognized it as more of a feeling than knowledge. It was familiar to him. It was what had come to him in his delusional state. Ash unstrapped himself and floated closer to the viewport—pain ignored. His hands flat on either side of the portal, he squinted, tilted his head sideways, opened his eyes wide, tried everything he could make the form more discernible. It seemed to resist his efforts to bring it into focus or even determine its edges. But it was definitely outside.

"Who are you?" Ash didn't think it odd that he should ask this, sincerely, to something outside the capsule and in the vacuum of space, or that he should ask "who" instead of "what." It seemed perfectly natural to him, like he might not receive an answer but he knew there was one, and that's what mattered. He couldn't sense a response. It seemed to drift outside. He had no sense of perspective—the form could have been small, human sized, and only a few meters away, or could have been the size of a planet and thousands of kilometers away. He had the understanding, though, that it was on the small side.

"What do you want?" No response.

Why is it, no . . . *she*, he recalled, staying outside? She wanted him to see something, figure something out. He eased back into the chair and strapped in without thinking about it, his eyes on the various screens and scanners on the console. He didn't think there was any way he could get reliable readings of anything with so many systems failing or on the verge of failing, but she was outside, whatever she wanted him to see was outside, so that's where he began. He initiated a complete scan around the craft. It took a long time for both the subsystems and himself to sort through the error garbage and find nothing out there. He looked back at the form in the darkness. Nothing physical, or nothing belonging to the first four dimensions. He started a dark matter/energy scan, a neutrino-arc scan, and a dimensional resonance scan, and a few others. Some of the scans he had to restart, others needed random intervention to keep going or get past unrecoverable errors. This was going to take a while.

After a half hour or so of sitting, occasionally typing or adjusting something, the pain started to seep back over his head. He was breaking apart, literally, and had been since he arrived at the end of the universe. Despite the shielding, he and the ship had been losing molecules, bonds between atoms weakening and breaking. He was thankful for the earlier reprieve from the suffering, but now with the pain starting to win again, he was looking forward to the final end. He started fading in and out of consciousness, trying to focus each time he resurfaced, to respond to new errors in the scanning processes and keep them going.

He woke up at some point; he didn't know how long he had been out this time—it felt like a while. His mouth was dry and his breathing shallow, but the pain had subsided once again to a dull agony throughout his body. She was gone from the viewport, but he felt her presence. She was back inside the capsule—she was keeping him alive, wanting him to finish something. He looked around and didn't see her, but he knew she was there.

Ash found the scanners had all completed their tasks at some point and were waiting for his examination. It took a while to analyze the findings, make sense of what he was discovering. Eventually, he was able to make sure the evidence shown wasn't an error, so what was left was figuring out what it meant. There was a near infinite energy well centered on his exact location.

Was it possible that he was on top of a remaining black hole's singularity? No, that didn't pan. The scans from the first two days didn't bear that out—whatever it is had formed since he had been there. If he were a resident of Flatland in a two-dimensional plane, he would say the well was under him, in his unperceived dimension of depth. This was something that seemed to exist outside the dozen dimensions of his universe, but not in an additional dimension—from somewhere altogether unconnected—was the only way he could make sense of the math. From somewhere "below" him, around him and inside him, a bulge of infinite energy was trying to push its way through the fabric to exist in the same space he occupied.

Then it made sense. Whether the numbers finally clicked, or she had something to do with it, he finally saw what was happening: A new universe, a younger sibling to his own in the family of the multiverse, was being drawn to the weakened warp he had created with his shielded craft. Another universe, co-existing with his own but in some nascent state, a state of pure energy, probably exactly like his own universe, was in the very beginning before it instantaneously expanded into whatever was there before it. A new universe that wanted to be born to replace the dead one; and his presence, accidental as it was, was the catalyst that would make it happen.

Except, there was a problem: His shield would collapse and the capsule disintegrate and his compressed time-space bubble would be eradicated before the critical mass down the well could be reached, allowing it to tear through. Even if he held it together, the warp he was creating in the tattered fabric of space and time might still not be enough to allow the proto-universe to burst through. He needed to accelerate the unraveling. Ash started playing with the numbers, running possibilities through the computer as fast as he could, the pain nearly forgotten. He was liminally aware of her presence near him.

Finally, just as he heard the first groan of weakening metal somewhere behind him, he found it. He found a way to funnel a controlled anti-matter failure cascade through the dark matter array and into the warp shield. The cascade would last a micro second, the entire process would be nearly instantaneous, and would obliterate the ship in the process even if it weren't currently being torn apart. But that instant would be all that was needed to tear open space and allow the infinitely compressed fabric of the alternate space to expand violently and gloriously into this dead one. He started the work to make it happen, unconsciously groaning and gritting through every movement.

When he was done, there was no time to wait: buckling had begun to appear in the bulkhead, the cabin lights finally failed after minutes of flickering on and off, the main console was barely working anymore. The shield was failing and the capsule in its last shudders, but Ash felt as though he had some kind of shield around himself as his own condition hadn't worsened during the work. Several times he felt certain he saw her out the corner of his eye, always a formless impression rather than something physical. A couple of times, after coming out of an intense focus on a task, he realized in retrospect that he had heard singing in the back of his mind. Now all he had to do was instigate the antimatter failure before it started on its own, when it was too late to do any good.

Ash stood at the last working terminal and held his finger over the unsecured button that would shut down containment. He looked outside. There was no mistaking her presence any longer, she was now a translucent, shimmering formlessness that was truly separate from the surrounding black yet still retained the quality of having undefined edges. Despite her luminance, he still found it difficult to determine where space ended and she began. He knew she was pleased. Was she what humanity eventually evolved into? Perhaps she was a creature from the future of the new universe, come back to see it born. Maybe she was truly something supernatural. He didn't know, and it saddened him to think he never would know for sure. But he knew that together they did this, together they would bring life back into the nothing. Brave? Noble? No, he was none of these things. He was content.

Ash pressed the button. The destruction of each stage of the process occurred one picosecond after the processes completed its intended function. The capsule, the bubble of ancient space-time, silently collapsed into a singularity as the tattered universe around it sent the blinding energy the event generated away in all directions. The singularity lasted only long enough to welcome the new universe as it instantaneously expanded through the opening and started the cooling process that would eventually give birth to new galaxies, stars, and worlds.

AT LEAST THERE'S NO TRAFFIC

Actor and writer Wil Wheaton, and award winning sci-fi author John Scalzi, set up a contest challenging people to write a fan-fic that explains this painting by artist Jeff Zugale below. So, I gave it a shot.

The style is a departure from my usual fare as the story embraces surrealist absurdity. But, look at the picture that inspired it—how could it not!?

The story contains many in-jokes that only fans of Wheaton and Scalzi are likely to get—but I think it should still be enjoyable as well to those who don't get it.

To see Jeff's illustration in all its gonzo full-color glory, see it at: http://artblog.jeffzugale.com/2010/05/sheer-madness-for-good-cause-with.html

* * * *

And so as I write this, the hordes are massing. This may be
"Master?"
This may be the final entry I write, dear reader.
"Master. . . ."
The pencil paused over the discolored page. Wil Wheaton

clenched his hands into fists. "What. What is it? I'm writing. You know I'm not to be disturbed when. I. Am. *Writing.*"

"I . . . there's a Scalzan at the gate, Master."

Wheaton sighed. "There are many Scalzans at the gate."

"I know, Master. What I mean is there's one requesting audience."

Wil turned the chair to face his servant. The creak and moan from the battered chair accentuated the tension in the broken room. "And what does the misshapen creature want?"

"He brings word from Lord Scalzi, Master."

"I'm sure it's too much to ask that it's a surrender."

"Master?"

"Nothing. I'll be right there."

"Yes, Master." The servant scurried away on four legs. Wil closed his eyes, flopped his head back, and sighed.

After a moment, he rubbed his eyes with the palms of his hands and turned back to his pages. He scribbled several more lines, read what he wrote, then shuffled the pages into a neat pile. Wil bound them with a rusty paperclip and placed the stack carefully in an accordion folder—each pocket marked with a month and each month sorted by dates. It was the only way he had left to remember what day it was. He wound the string around the grommet, securing the folder shut, then placed it carefully in front of the row of similar folders on the shelf.

Shaking out the cramps in his hand, Wil crossed the expansive room with one and a half walls left standing and descended the staircase to the main hall. He hadn't cared that the room he chose as his study was more a rooftop than a room—it no longer rained and the view of the glowing pyroclastic flows in the everlasting night was inspiring. Plus, the ravine that encircled the gated community he and his people lived in kept his building at a safe distance from Scalzian catapult and trebuchet attacks. The room could actually be quite peaceful at times.

He reached the cracked marble ground floor and checked

his posture. Tall, stern . . . good. Breathing controlled. Hand on his side— no, in his pocket. No, on the banister. Good. He nodded to the doormen. They lifted the bar and one of them pulled open the left-side door revealing a stocky, orange and green mottled figure in scale armor made from soup cans. "Enter." Wil's voiced boomed impressively in the stark chamber.

The once human creature walked at a casual pace to the center of the room. His grin revealed a row of teeth broken off at the gum-line. "I have a message for you from The Great and Terrible Lord High Scalzi."

"Really? That's what he's using?" The question was rhetorical but Wil paused regardless. "Why couldn't he have just sent it over the wall with the last barrage of useless junk?"

"Lord High Scalzi, in his graciousness, thought you would appreciate the . . . human touch." The messenger sniggered at his own expense.

Wil sighed. "Fine. Let's hear it and be done with it."

"Indeed. Lord High Scalzi wishes to grant you one last opportunity to hand over Rancho Stucko Estates and all properties within its confines, else he shall take it by force."

And there it was. The final, formal declaration he'd been waiting weeks to receive. No more targeted strikes, surprise raids, hours long bombardments. Scalzi was getting as tired with this siege as he and was going to make a final, all-out strike with his army.

"When?"

"In one hour."

Crap! Now *that* was unexpected; though, really, not surprising. Wil had been keeping his forces on alert the last several days, expecting either a warning such as this followed by a day to consider and worry, or no warning at all. Deep breath . . . but not *too* deep. Don't look flummoxed—just calm.

Wil strode to the messenger in measured strides. "You tell your Lame and Ridiculous Mister Stoned Scalzi that I have received his message, and he is welcome to come and try to take my lands if he thinks he can. You tell him I think if he had the ability, he'd have done so by now instead of wasting my time with his annoying pea-shooters."

The messenger cackled and said, "Lord High Scalzi said you'd posture like a boy playing king—"

Wil closed the last few feet between them, grabbed the messenger by the single, wood-like horn protruding from the side of the shocked man-creature's skull, and pulled his head down to poise his right eye over the tip of the sharpened pencil in Wil's right hand. "I ought to kill you right here and now and throw your corpse back at Scalzi as my answer."

The messenger licked his lips and cleared his throat. "I would be happy to deliver your reply verbally." His putrid, infected breath wafted up to Wil's nose and he grimaced in reflex. Wil continued to hold the creature's head over the pencil for a beat, then threw him from his grasp. He wiped his hand on his shirt as the messenger recovered from stumbling.

"Out of my sight," Wil waved him off and turned his back to him. He heard the man chuckle, no hint of fear or anxiety. Wil closed his eyes and listened to the receding footsteps and the barring of the door. He took a deep breath . . . exhale.

He turned back to the hall, "Sandra!"

"Here, Master." A tall, rubbery figure stepped from the shadows. Her skin was as black as what she'd stepped from, her hair flowed behind her like a silk cape. "Your orders?"

"Ready all forces. Make sure there are scouts at length along the wall to watch for flanking attacks, but keep it as small as possible. I need all available troops in ranks at the front gate. We shall meet them on the field."

"Yes, Master." She began to slip away.

"Sandra."

"Master?"

"Also, ready Fluffy Bitterpants. I shall ride her into battle."

"Master." She was gone.

Wil mashed the palms of his hands into his eyes and shook his head. He climbed back up the stairs, already battle worn.

* * * *

Wil stood in at the edge of the floor, his foot crumbling dust and splinters off to the ground below. The voice behind him was hollow but comforting. "So, this is it?"

He nodded, still looking out at the distant land that was once urban sprawl at the foot of rolling hills, now a burned and twisted wasteland. "I believe so."

The voice waited. Then said, "You have doubts?"

"I do, LeVar. I don't mind saying."

"You *are* ready."

"Am I? How can I be ready for this?" He turned to face his friend. LeVar's ghostly, translucent form wavered and floated off the floor. He was dressed in a casual suit, stylish beard, and half a banana hairclip apparently carpet-stapled to his face. His smoky eyes peered from behind the ragged teeth of the half clip. Wil scowled, as usual (he couldn't help himself), and continued, "How can anyone be ready for this? Nothing in my experience, my background, has prepared me for any of this. Not The Shower, not The Change, not a writer-turned-orc and his misshapen army of whatevers attacking me."

"And not prepared to be a lord over a domain, either, no?"

"No."

LeVar smiled. "And yet, here you are. For the last two years, successfully leading scores of your own people and misshapen whatevers through adversity and strife, to live in relative harmony."

"It's easy when the alternative is, . . ." he waved his hand at the distant volcanoes.

"Wil," LeVar tried to put his hand on Wil's shoulder but it passed through. He seemed to not notice, "You *are* capable. These people trust you; they rely on you. They are about to do battle for, and with, you. They are *your* horde. You earned them."

Wil dipped his head and shook it. "I don't know. Maybe."

"What choice do you have?"

He looked at LeVar and his chagrined smile. He chuckled. "Well, if there's nothing else, I guess there's that for motivation."

LeVar nodded. "By the way, where's Anne?"

"Gone."

"Oh, God, you don't mean—"

"No! Oh, no. No. I had the boys take her up to New Doctorow when things started to head the way, well, it's become."

"I see. Good."

"Ever since she turned into a window box of marigold, it's been hard on her, you know."

"Yeah, I know." He nodded sympathetically.

"LeVar."

"Hmm?"

"You'll be there, with me, in the battle won't you?"

LeVar smiled. "Wil, my friend. I may not be able to fight, but I'll always be there with you. No matter what."

Wil felt a weight lift from him. "Thank you."

A loud, clear horn echoed through the buildings. "Formation's ready," Wil said. "I better finish getting dressed."

He put on The Sweater then pulled a trench coat over his shoulders. "Say, LeVar. You know, I've been meaning to ask you. . . ."

"Hmm?"

"About the visor—"

"Oh fuck you!"

"I, wha?"

"Like you think you're the only one with coping issues? You're the only one with a past to deal with?"

"I— I don't . . . what?"

"You know we *all* had to get past it, all of us. But do you care? Oh, no. You write a geek book and become a beloved hero and what happens to us? You know Jonathan cried on my shoulder? *Cried on my shoulder.* Said, 'I never wanted to direct, you know.' He said, 'I always wanted to be a dancer!'"

"What— I don't— What's that supposed to—"

"Screw you, Wil Wheaton!"

"I was just wondering—" there was a pop of air and Wil was speaking to an empty room. "Wondering why the staples, since you're frakking ethereal."

Wil stood in the middle of the room. The distant buzz of assembled troops floated over the steady bass sound of rumbling volcanoes.

"Well, crap." He tied the coat's belt and strode to the stairs.

* * * *

The full moon cut through the clouds and ambient glow from the lava, bathing the field and the armies on either end with a silver sheen. At Wil's back was his home—one of the last remaining clusters of buildings within sight. Ahead of him, behind the enemy, was a craggy valley where Scalzi and his followers lived. If that was living.

The enemy. They were like a "Best Of" from the paintings of Hieronymus Bosch. Wil looked to either side of him; his army was pretty much the same except with more pastels. The Change was not kind. At least, not to most. Wil felt truly fortunate to have escaped The Change with virtually no effect. He wished the tail could have at least been prehensile, but it could have been worse. It could always be worse.

Scalzi had a horn blower send a call, and then began walking across the field, alone. Wil, not yet mounted, began walking as well. Then he turned to the little triangular-shaped fellow standing behind him.

"You have the box?"

The triangle squire lifted his torn Snuggie to show an iron box hanging from a chain around the middle of his body, just under where his face and beak protruded. "Yes, Master."

"Good. Ready it."

"Yes, Master," he said, and began to unlock the box. Wil turned back to Scalzi and continued walking.

They met at the middle. Scalzi smiled. "Old friend."

"Bite me."

Scalzi's smile melted easily into a scowl. He scanned the army at Wil's back. "Not much."

"It'll be enough, John." Scalzi winced at the name.

"You'd be wise to give up now."

"I thought you already gave me a last chance. What's this? Nervous about my calling your bluff?"

"Oh, Wil Wil Wil. What a performance. The role of a lifetime! Savior of the masses? Or are we looking at more of a last stand of Davy Crockett? You know, you kind of look like what I'd think Davy looked like."

"You're overplaying your hand, John. I've more outs than you."

"What you have, boy, is a crappy little hamlet that's about to be repainted with your blood!"

"You don't even belong here! What are you doing here, John? This was my home. *My* home."

"I can't help where I was stuck when The Shower and The Change happened."

"Oh, wah. There's the real John. I knew he was there. The whiny little-man inside a green costume." It was his own bluff. Wil was terrified of this man, this orc-thing who was *once* a man, who had intimidated him even before The Change. John Scalzi had been a kind, generous, force of nature who had since pared that list down to one remaining quality. In truth, Wil had no idea how many outs he had. He was now playing the man, not the cards.

No final words, no insult. Scalzi turned and marched back to his line, leaving Wil standing alone. He turned and made way for his own line, certain the entire way he could feel the force of an axe or a spear screaming toward his back.

Wil walked to his battle cat, Fluffy Bitterpants. She purr-meowed and shifted her wings at his approach. He scratched her neck with both hands and pressed his forehead against her's, below her single horn. After a moment, he took the reins from her stable girl, grabbed the saddle, and lifted himself onto her back. He was in the best shape of his life, he mused, and he wasn't going to have the opportunity to really enjoy it.

Wil untied the coat belt, took hold the lapels, and in a deliberate mix of casual and the dramatic, pulled the coat open and off his shoulders—revealing the red and blue grotesquery on his chest. The colorful visage in rictus served as a totem of power to his own people, drawing gasps of awe and shouts of fervor. From the other side of the field came grunts and cries of hate and, hopefully, dread.

Scalzi, shield on one arm now, held his other fist high into the air, waving strips of something brown. He yelled in a voice that boomed across the field and carried over the cracking of volcanoes, "*I eat your bacon! I eat it up!*" He took an angry bite out of whatever he was holding.

The stable girl, still standing next to Wil, cocked her head, "I didn't think there were any pigs left—" Wil stopped her with a slow shake of his head. She put her hand over her mouth.

Someone held his spear out to him; he took it, hefted it, and held it point up as he maneuvered Fuffy Bitterpants around to face his troops.

He scanned the line and weighed them each in his sight. After a pause, he began in a growing voice, "I could give you a speech. I could invoke the words of great generals and leaders of men. But that would not give you any more courage than I know you already have. That would not give you all the strength, the will, and the valiant righteousness, of a people whose homes and families and way of life are being attacked by ruthless interlopers." The faces of his troops, ranging from the normal to the truly horrifying, stared back at him in reverent attention. In some, he saw fear—in most, he saw determination. A couple he saw featureless blank ovals. (He never could get used to that.) "Know then, you are fighting not just for yourselves, but for the lives of your wives, husbands, children . . . all of our very futures. You fight . . . for great justice!"

A cheer erupted from the men and women, and other things, throughout the ranks. Swords clanged on shields, clubs banged on the ground. Fluffy Bitterpants pawed the ground and growled.

It was time.

Wil turned his mount around, back toward the Scalzans, who were cheering and clamoring in equal measure. Wil nodded at the triangle squire. He nodded back and pushed the play button on the boom-box powered by the six D-cells that had been kept safe in the iron box. The plastic speakers were replaced by PA speakers and prepared to blast his carefully chosen battle music across the field.

He held his spear up high, Fluffy Bitterpants reared back, ready to spring when the first, thunderous notes exploded—

We're no strangers to love,
You know the rules and so do I.

"Oh sonuva—!"

"Sorry! Sorry." The squire frantically pressed track buttons and the high-frequency sound of the CD player scanning along the tracks whined through the PA. "OK, got it. Sorry."

Wil's face was in his palm when the intended music shattered the uncomfortable silence. He sighed and mumbled, "Whatever." And charged.

I can see a new horizon underneath the blazin' sky
I'll be where the eagle's flying higher and higher
Gonna be your man in motion, all I need is a pair of wheels
Take me where my future's lyin', St. Elmo's Fire

THE SWORD REMEMBERS

This is the oldest story in this collection, written sometime during my undergrad days. Years later, during the grad school days in which all of these works saw their creation, I took this story out of the personal slush and found it still spoke to me, I felt warm and wonderful thoughts as I read it, and I knew I just had to do what was needed to allow it into the light of day. It wanted life. In fact, I think Sarah, the narrator, has more she needs to say.

None of us was surprised by the flash or the thunder; the body that fell from the sky, though, was unexpected. It didn't fall far, maybe four feet. We were expecting lightning, or fire, or even swarms of three-eyed monkeys—but when I saw Laonid also looking perplexed, I knew the surprise appearance was not *his* doing.

Jon, being the kind of person to act first and let someone else think later, was first to shrug off the event. He threw his axe directly at Laonid's chest. As expected, it bounced off the magician's invisible shielding. This time, however, it was just enough of an added distraction following the odd body appearance that Laonid stumbled and didn't react as fast as he should have. This gave me the opportunity to move in with Scarab, my blessed dagger, and cut through the magician's shielding—and throat. I held onto the dagger as Laonid pulled it down to the ground with his collapse. I gave it a quick turn for good measure, then jerked it out and let his lifeless body fall beside the one that recently appeared. Eager sparks of energy jumped off the mage's body and disappeared into the air as the flesh gave up the gift of magic as it was already giving up its heat.

I looked around. Jon was picking up his axe; Terrin was sitting against a nearby tree, pressing a wadded cloth against his bleeding face; and our new guest lay at my feet. I knelt close, as I re-bound my fallen hair into the leather band, to see if this fellow was any livelier than Laonid and watched the stranger's chest move shallowly but regularly. That was something. Life established, I examined his appearance: Odd clothing—too clean and well tailored to be one of us, a commoner, yet too flimsy and simple to be well-born. He had no armor, weapon, or tool on him to confirm what his clean, soft face and hands already told me—he was neither a soldier nor laborer. He *must* be well-born. Perhaps he was recently robbed of the rest of the clothing people like him tended to wear.

"Terrin," I called out looking up and over the stranger. He was gingerly touching at the edges of the slice on his cheek. At my hail he snapped to and came over to kneel next to me.

"So, what have we here, Sarah? Obviously not an illusion."

I nodded. "He lives too. Out cold. His hair and skin make him out as a Northerner, beyond the Range, but his clothing seem much more suited to the warmth of the southern lands."

"He doesn't exactly have the build of a Northerner. Do you think he might have been robbed?" I smiled and told Terrin that had been my guess as well.

Jon finished tapping Laonid with his toe and came over beside us. "Did the spell-slinger there create it or something else-" and that's when the stranger decided to wake up, screaming. Even Jon was startled and backed up a step. Poor Terrin had yelped and rolled back off his heels, flopping ungracefully in the dirt. My reaction was somewhere between the two. The stranger stopped and took a breath, then for the first time looked around at us. He looked as if he wasn't quite sure what he was seeing, also looked a little scared. I had to feel bad for him: wherever he came from, he had been doing something somewhere far away and was suddenly whisked here surrounded by people he'd never met. I almost remembered to what it was like when I first encountered the unusual and unexpected myself. Many years ago. Almost.

Terrin had lifted himself to his elbows and rose up beside the stranger. The man watched Terrin, his eyes constantly looking at the gash in my companion's face that had started bleeding again. "Don't be frightened; we're not going to harm you. What's your name? Where do you come from?"

The stranger looked at him, then back at Jon and me before resting his gaze back at Terrin. For a moment I was afraid he couldn't understand until he replied, "M-my name is Randy. Randy Collins. I, well, I'm from Kansas City." I looked to Terrin, and Jon, both shrugged at each. "Where am I? How'd . . . how did . . . where am I?" he stammered as he looked about himself. He still had the look of someone that had just woken up and was unsure if he was still dreaming.

"Well, you're just outside the town of Fade," I began. The stranger scowled. "Which is near the High Woods." He continued scowling. "In the Kingdom of Dellerin," and that's when he looked decidedly shocked.

"Kingdom? What do you mean *'Kingdom'*?" None of us was sure how to answer that. "Last I remember I was hiking through the woods and then *bam*! A white light . . . and, and then I was here."

Jon tried to help with, "Look, let's cut to it. This bastard," he tapped the body with his foot, again, "evidently tried to cast something nasty at us. Instead he. . . ."

"Summoned," Terrin offered.

"Yeah, summoned you from wherever you came from by mistake. Which allowed us to kill him. The bastard." He tapped the body with his toe again for clarification, in case we forgot who he was referring to.

"I . . . but, I, . . ." Randy kept looking back and forth among us. When he fainted, I think we were relieved.

* * * *

By the time darkness set in we had camp set up on the edge of the woods. The fire was roaring; Laonid's body was wrapped up and prepared with a preservation potion for the trip back to Wizard's Rock; and Randy was clutching himself in a ball, staring into the flames.

Terrin passed him a hare's leg. "I just don't get it," Randy continued, "I mean, how can a person be zapped into a whole other universe like that? I just don't get it."

I sighed and accepted some food from Terrin. "Thank you, squire," I joked.

"Certainly, fair wench," he responded as usual. I smiled at him. Turning to Randy, "So you don't have magic in your world."

Randy shook his head. "Well, we have entertainers that do things that *look* like magic, but I mean, well, it's not *really* magic."

"We have magic here," I began, feeling melancholy for some reason. "We have wizards, we have curses, we have curse'd wizards. And one of those wizards brought you here." I paused to chew and think. "Granted, it was an accident on his part, but here you are."

"And what are we going to do with you?" Terrin finished for me.

Randy looked up from the leg he was delicately nibbling on, "What do you mean? I mean, c'mon. I *have* to go back! You have to send me back. I can't stay here—I have a job and family and friends and the next Robert Jordan book to read and . . . and, . . ." I watched his eyes start to moist, his breath hitch. I tried to imagine what it would be like to lose my family and get ripped from my homeland . . . and every time I'm a little startled to remember that *did* happen to me. I felt a little bad for him.

"Well," Terrin began thoughtfully, "We *are* going to Wizard's Stone, after all. The very seat of the Wizard's Council. I would be surprised if one of the Council couldn't send you back. I mean, if this hedgewizard can bring you here, then surely one of the archwizards can send you back." He looked at me for reassurance.

I paused, then nodded agreement. "It's only a few days from here, and we already have an audience with them to present Laonid's body."

Jon had come back from checking on the horses by this time and dropped a small, sheathed sword at Randy's feet. Randy looked down, beaming smile turned to confusion—an expression that has become natural for him by that time. "Uhm, what's this?"

"A sword," Jon answered as he pulled some meat off the spit and sat on the log next to him. "Hope you know how to use it." He glanced at Randy's arms and raised a skeptical eyebrow. Randy just looked at the sword at his feet.

"Uh, why should I need to know how to use this?" The three of us looked at each other, wondering who was going to tell him.

Jon looked a little amused as he said, "Because, in order to get back to Wizard's Stone we'll have to go near a goblin bandit camp." After another look at Randy's arms, "You might want to go practice on a tree over there." Randy looked back up at him, and we weren't at all surprised to see him faint again.

* * * *

"**A**nd then if you mix salt in with the coal. No, wait. Salt's not right. No, it is, but . . . OH! Yeah, saltpeter. That's right. Yeah it sounds funny, but if you mix that with the coal and the bird . . . crap, you get gun powder. I think. I don't even know what saltpeter *is*, come to think of it."

Randy had been talking like that for the entire day. Ever since he woke up that morning all he talked about were things of his home world and how to make items. At first we were glad he was in a good mood and cheerful. It seemed after a decent night's sleep he'd decided spending a few days in an alternate world from his own would be exciting. Like, "a fantasy novel come true" is how he put it. Unfortunately, he kept going on about how he could be our world's "scientific hero," passing his knowledge of advanced technology unto our primitive world. It was downhill from there.

"But then you'd have to have some really strong metal tubes that will take the explosion and . . . uhm, do you have steel?"

Terrin drew his sword before Randy's wide eyes, "What does this look like? Wood?"

"Yeah, ok. So then what you'd need-"

"Shh!" Jon halted his horse; the rest of us did the same, except Randy had a little trouble. He was riding the pack mule and his complete lack of horsemanship was getting on the normally docile animal's nerves. We listened intently. Jon, our expert at all things green or furry and knew the forest better than any of the rest of us, "We're near where we encountered them last time."

"Last time?" Randy said, but I shh'd him. After a short pause, he tried again but in a strained whisper, "You'd already met these goblins? What happened?" Jon waved him up next to him. After Randy managed to get the mule to walk forward a bit, Jon took the reigns and slowly led Randy about twenty feet up the barely used road that cut through the forest. He looked off the left side of the road for a moment then pointed. Randy looked to where Jon was pointing and I could see him pale from yards away. Terrin and I moved up next to them and saw the leg Jon had lopped off a goblin two days earlier still lying in the grass, collecting quite a swarm of flies.

Jon lifted his hand, although no one was talking. We all strained our ears trying to hear what Jon had heard. We didn't have to wait long. Each of us drew our swords—Randy hesitantly. We heard some noises in the distance, feet crunching through the brush. As the source of the sound came closer I watched Randy appear to get himself emotionally prepared, then more nervous as the sounds grew louder.

Out of the trees from the right walked two goblins carrying bared swords. One of them looked battered, but I don't remember which one of us had fought him. The other, if I recall, was some captain of sorts. We didn't exactly make introductions last time. The captain stopped at the side of the road and made what sounded like laughter. I glanced at Randy who stared in fright, or shock. I couldn't really tell.

"Humans come back do they? Forget kill some of us?" He laugh-growled again. None of us spoke. "Go on, ride-way that way and leave us. None left to kill. Go on . . . go." He was waving us off with his sword. I looked over to Terrin, and we both looked to Jon. His eyes narrowed and without turning his gaze away nudged his mount to walk on. We all followed, careful to keep our swords ready. Randy looked confused, but I could see a certain amount of hesitant relief. None of us took our eyes off the goblins at the side of the road until we had turned a curve and could no longer see them.

I rode up next to Jon, "What do you think? Last time I counted only three, maybe four goblins running off."

"I've known goblins to flee a losing battle, but I don't recall one turning down the opportunity for revenge." Randy remained refreshingly silent, though I could understand his fear. He was listening to Jon intently. Jon continued, "The leader seemed too friendly. For a goblin, *any* friendly is. . . ."

In a whisper Randy asked, "So, are you saying, it might be a trap?" As if in response an arrow with black and green fletching appeared from nowhere out of Jon's arm, accompanied by two or three more that passed overhead. He yelled in both pain and anger and charged his horse forward. Before following, I looked at where I thought the arrow had come from but didn't see anything.

We got maybe twenty yards before four spear wielding goblins charged from the brush. Jon's mount received a glancing hit, but Jon had already leapt off and barreled toward the goblin. The rest of us, except Randy, also dismounted and entered combat. They had evidently intended to do some real damage with the spears while we were on horseback, but fortunately the goblins weren't very skillful with them in hand-to-hand.

Jon had already killed the goblin that wounded his horse and engaged another when I looked back at him. I parried a stab from one and grabbed the spear with my other hand. I tried to wrench it from his grip but he had a good grasp on it. So instead I pulled on it hard to bring him right in front of me and took a good swing at his neck. He tried to duck, but not in time. My blade bit deep into his skull, sending him straight to the ground and taking my sword with him. He lay there twitching as I placed a foot on his head to lever my sword out.

I heard Terrin yell, "Die, goblin dung!" and I turned in time to watch him run his opponent through. And to see an arrow appear from out of his back. I turned back down the road and saw three more goblin running toward us. They dropped their bows and drew swords as they ran. Jon started running to meet them, and Terrin passed me with the arrow bobbing in his back. I was glad to see he wasn't downed. I ran as well.

Jon got there first which meant he had to parry attacks from two goblins at the same time before Terrin and I got there. We reached the third goblin simultaneously, and in one of those rare instances when everything seems to work just right, both of us got right through the goblin's attack. I slashed its gut while Terrin sliced off its head, and kept going.

One of the two remaining goblins was clutching its fountaining throat and stumbling away, the other one had a chance to parry Jon's lunge but didn't even see the stab in the kidney (I think goblins have kidneys) Terrin gave it. It screamed and dropped its sword. I could see Jon's distaste as he made the killing blow. Even against someone who would still kill him if they could, Jon hated striking an unarmed assailant. Just one of his quirks I admired him for.

The three of us looked down the road to see the captain. He stood a moment then limped into the woods. I turned to Terrin while Jon, also limping, came up to us. I saw Jon had a gash in his leg, bleeding pretty badly, but it didn't look like it was in a life-threatening place. "Hey, Ter'," Jon said, "You know you have an arrow in your back?"

Terrin tried to look over his shoulder and winced in pain. "Yeah, I thought something like that. It's going to hurt like a bansidhe pretty soon here. Hey look," he said turning his back to Jon, "Matching arrows." He laughed and the end of the arrow bounced at the movement. We heard the mule bray behind us, and we turned in time to see Randy, still clutching the sword against his chest, faint off the beast.

* * * *

I was finishing treating Terrin's wound by the time Randy finally said anything. The arrow had hit the bottom edge of Terrin's shoulder blade and stopped, making the wound more or less superficial, as arrow wounds go. The tips didn't seem poisoned but I had kept an eye on Terrin and Jon's behavior for a couple of hours just to be sure.

"How, uhm, how often does things like that happen?" We all turned, surprised by Randy's sudden recovery. We'd been sure he was going to stutter and stammer as soon as he came to, but that had been a couple of hours before. After making sure he wasn't hurt from the fall, we flopped Randy over my horse, in front of the saddle, and rode far enough to make sure we were well out of goblin territory before setting up camp. Since Randy had woken up he'd sat quietly and watched the fire while the rest of us joked and chatted the stress and rush of battle out of our systems.

Terrin pulled his shirt back on with a wince, "Well, only whenever we travel outside of the city. There are goblins or ogres here and there. Bandits and undead. And a lot of worse things. We've been through a lot more than this before."

Randy looked thunderstruck. "I . . . don't know what to say. I mean, I was thinking this morning how . . . exciting being an adventurer would be." Jon snorted as he stirred the stew.

"It certainly is exciting," I agreed. "But anyone who seeks the life of the sword for the excitement certainly doesn't last long. Most of us venture through the wildlands because it's the only way we know to make a living. Some are forced into it by necessity. Some by a calling."

There was a silence that lasted several minutes. Jon tossed me an oilcloth for my sword. Terrin started mixing some more herbs that lessened his and Jon's pains. Jon tended the stew while staring into the fire. Randy also stared into the fire, still clutching the sword. Jon had asked for the sword back while camp was being set up, but Randy hadn't responded. Jon shrugged and went on. He was probably a little disgusted at Randy's performance earlier. Or lack of.

Finally, Randy broke the silence: "I just didn't expect it to be like that. So . . . fast. So . . . gory." No one looked at him, but his remark did make me remember the blood and violence I had put out of my mind. That I had gotten very good at putting out of my mind.

I had been feeling uneasy since the day before, since Randy's arrival. I had tried to put that out of my mind as well, but it kept gnawing at me. Growing and seething into my consciousness until I just couldn't ignore it any further, and Randy's resent observations weren't making it any better. I couldn't sit there any longer.

"I'm going for a walk. Back later." I stood as I sheathed my sword and headed out into the thinning woods back toward where I knew the river was close by.

* * * *

I found a good place where a bend in the river spawned a creek running through some rocks banked by trees. The canopy was thin enough here to let the moon light my way.

I undid my hair and removed my boots, breeches, and shirt, and sunk myself into the cool water. I dunked under to get my face and hair wet, and began scrubbing; first with a cloth, then with my fingernails, despite having cut them short. I hadn't felt this unclean in years and something about both Randy's arrival and his last comment had made me sensitive to these feelings all over again. I scrubbed my arms, face, scalp, and chest raw, and didn't realize I was crying until I noticed I couldn't see. I stopped scrubbing and held my face in my hands, shamed, and perhaps trying to hide my sobbing from watchers who I knew weren't there. I was by myself, and I cried for that too. I had forgotten how alone I was and right then I hated Randy for having reminded me.

After some time I calmed down and sat on a rock, letting the water flow around my body. It felt both cold and calming against my sore skin. I still felt stunned by how sudden and strong my emotions exploded, and just breathed in the night air, looking at how the moon's reflection rippled on the water.

I sat there for some time, doing a good job not thinking about anything, when I heard someone approach. I thought it was Jon or Terrin coming to look for me, so I just sat and waited. When I heard Randy say, "Oh, sorry, I uh, didn't know you were na-, bathing. I'll leave," I actually moved to cover myself. It was too dark to see anything, even so, I had never been modest. At least, not for years. When you live and work so closely with a couple of men who you think of as brothers and who treat you as their sister, modesty simply became a non-issue. I caught myself and relaxed again.

"No, that's OK, go ahead and sit down." I felt bad that, shortly before, I had such hateful feelings toward Randy when it wasn't really his fault. Randy sat on a rock by the edge of the water, with his back to it, looking toward where he'd came from. We sat in silence for a few minutes, Randy uncomfortably. After a while he turned around, as if afraid he'd disturb me, to face me. His feet dangled above the water; I just sat and looked out and up at the stars.

"What about you?"

I looked at him, "I'm sorry?"

"What about you? Why are you out here? Doing what you're doing?"

I thought it was an odd and obvious question. Then I remembered what we had last discussed at the fire and I felt resentful that after I had purged and re-repressed my feelings, he'd brought that back up. But I felt too empty right then to let it become more than just a shadow of a real emotion. I just sighed and let it pass over me.

Then I let myself think about it. At first just barely touching the edges of the question for fear of bringing the emotions back, but I didn't have to worry. I was pretty well drained. "Hmm. What about me." When the wind wasn't blowing the water too much, you could see the reflections of the stars. "I haven't thought much about myself in a long time. I guess I'm one of those who had no other choice." I could feel him looking at me, curious. I continued, mainly to myself: "I suppose I *did* have a choice but it was between living on the street, selling my body, or taking up the sword. I didn't have connections or a family to get me into university, I wasn't apprenticed to anyone, and I basically had no future. I was a nobody in a place that wasn't kind to nobodies. At some point, I don't recall when, I was half forced into doing some things I wasn't very proud of, to say the least, and was surprised to find that I was good at fighting."

"Well," I dismissed, "it's a long story." Once I started talking I kept going despite my desire to stay private. "The final result, here I am. For years I've convinced myself that I was doing all I could do, all I was allowed to do, and put the . . . the consequences out of my head. I hadn't thought in a very long time about what I wanted to do or be, and now I've started thinking again how this certainly wasn't what I had in mind.

"Funny how life works."

After a pause, he replied quietly, "Yeah. It is."

We sat in silence for a while. The sound of the water against the rocks, frogs in the grass, a whippoorwill in the distance. My skin tingled in a both itchy and oddly pleasant way.

"I certainly didn't expect this," He said. I snorted, amused. He continued, "I mean I guess no one expects to suddenly be whisked to another . . . universe or whatever, but this is some world right out of a fantasy book. So I guess you know, I expected monsters and magic and swords and stuff . . . but, it's so real. I mean, those goblins, they looked almost human." I hadn't said anything but he answered himself as if I had contradicted, "Well, I know not human. I mean, they have green leather-like skin and little horns and claws and stuff. But well, they could talk and think and frown. . . . Strange, that an expression would make me consider them more human than anything else. Even more than the talking. When I saw that one you killed almost right in front of me, when it frowned as if it knew what was coming and was disappointed and mad and sad at the same time, I don't know. I can't explain it."

"You don't have to." I tried to keep my eyes on one star's reflection in particular but my sight kept wavering.

After another silence Randy chuckled, "You know, in uh, fantasy novels, midnight bathing in clear streams tend to become romantic." He chuckled again, as if to say, *isn't that just silly*, but still hoping he might be right. I smiled, I couldn't help myself. After the past hour or so of dark brooding, this was just too cute. I looked up at Randy and considered for a second the world where people lived mundane lives and the only exciting thing that happened for them was what happened to other people in books. I'd forgotten what that kind of world was like. I chuckled myself, but for a different reason.

I stood up out of the water and walked onto one of the dry rocks, letting the moonlit water run off my body. I knew I was attractive by how others treated me, but I never considered it much. I walked over to my clothes making sure not to look at Randy who I knew was looking at me, probably a little stunned and surprised. I pulled my clothes on and loosely laced my shirt, which stuck to me since I didn't have anything to dry off with. I smiled softly as I walked over to Randy and with sincerity and tenderness I told him, "Never, ever, take for granted what little things you're given," and kissed his cheek. I carried my boots through the trees back to camp.

* * * *

The next day my sympathetic feelings for Randy had pretty much withered away.

We allowed him to ride the mule not just because of the blisters he was forming on his feet but because it forced him to be the closest to Laonid's body on the litter the mule dragged. The rest of us walked ahead of them by a few yards.

"I'm sorry," he said for perhaps the sixth or sixteenth time. "I really didn't know it would do that."

We'd been walking for almost an hour since the horses ran off. The forest was sparse but that just meant we had to separate now and then to check out paths through the trees one of them could have run through. Jon recovered his horse not far from where they ran off, but he chose to walk with Terrin and me until we found ours—despite his leg wound. Good cleaning, binding, and some herbal salve kept away the swelling and a lot of the pain, but I'm sure even for an experienced soldier it had to hurt.

"I really didn't know. I'd almost forgotten I had my cell phone with me until this morning. I was just seeing if it would pick something up, some signal. I mean, I knew, I guess, that it wouldn't, but I had to try." I could just get the jist of what he was saying. "I was just going through menu options and had no idea the 'Ode to Joy' alarm was set so loud. . . ."

The amazingly annoying, weird, loud sound that came out of his device startled all of us—most of all the horses. Even these well-trained beasts couldn't help but panic. If we'd been mounted we'd have been able to calm them immediately, but as it was, we were just getting ready to leave our mid-day camp. Jon's Thunder was the most battle experienced of our horses so his brief flight was probably just to fit in with the other two, I mused.

But that wasn't the worst. We knew we'd catch up with our horses: they would eventually stop and perhaps drink from the river that this old road ran along. They had probably run as far as they had mainly for the exercise once the initial surprise wore off. The worst was that Laonid's litter was lashed to Terrin's saddle. When his Ash ran off, she dragged the litter a fair distance, including through a small creek just off the path. It eventually snagged and the long cords that tethered it to the saddle snapped.

The nice thing about preservation potions is that all you have to do is sprinkle it onto the body you don't want to decompose for a few days. However, if it gets wet, whatever it should have decomposed in the time since it was first applied catches up all at once. It had been rather warm and sunny these last two days.

As I expected, we found Ash and Chicken Soup, (long story—I might tell it another time), grazing not much farther up. They looked at us as if to say, "Well there you are, snails. It's about time. Are we ready to go now?" I rubbed Chick'Soup's nose and checked her tack. All was well. She could smell Laonid, but didn't do anything more than snort and flick her ears. She was much more used to death than she was to loud, weird alarms.

After saddling up, Randy tried to apologize again. A look from Jon made him mumble it into a silence that lasted for the rest of the afternoon.

Some time later I started feeling sorry for him again. I'd occasionally look back over my shoulder and see him bob on the mule's back, looking down and sullen.

The trees had already been thin most of the day, but then they ended all at once giving way to large expanses of rolling land and wildflowers. Most of what could be seen was wild wheat and flax, weeds, and long grasses, but there was an occasional copse of dark green bush and a tree or two. The sky was a light blue and the clouds were unmoving wisps across the sky. It felt good. The sun was behind us and we could look out at the hills in the distance without having to squint or cover our eyes.

We'd all been silent since regaining our mounts, but I suppose Terrin felt the same uplifted spirit I did, and started to sing something quietly. I hadn't heard this one before and it was in the Northern tongue, I couldn't understand it, but it sounded like something between a ballad and a drinking song. A ballad about drinking, perhaps? I chuckled to myself.

I looked back at Randy: he was looking out to the fields to the right. I caught his eye and he looked at me. In a surprising act of rare silliness, I stuck my tongue out at him and smiled. He looked stricken at first then smiled back. I think I blushed at my own uncharacteristic behavior, and I turned back to the front, a little puzzled, but not at all bad. The sun warmed my hair and the fragrance of Spring grew stronger when I closed my eyes.

We reached the inn just after nightfall. We'd started seeing farms along the road a couple of hours before and knew we weren't far from Boarderdale: the small community just west of Daerwoe, where Wizard's Stone is. We'd have to stay in the inn for the night but we could be in Daerwoe proper before mid-morning the next day—even with a good long sleep.

Luckily, Terrin was able to purchase a preservation potion from the stable master. I would have been surprised if we couldn't get another one as it's custom to bury one's dead here in the Middlelands and, during the winter, the ground is frozen for many weeks on end. Sometimes most of the entire season. Terrin had Randy help him with its application. When they finished they joined me and Jon in the main room. Randy looked pale and shaky and there was a silent agreement among us all that he'd paid his penance. Terrin bought himself and Randy a couple of ales and joined us at a table next to the fire.

I had already arranged with the 'keep for lodgings for the night. Across from us on the other side of the large fireplace was a duo playing light music on a dulcimer and pipe. The scattering of locals talked to them between songs in a familiar manner implying the performers were also local and not minstrels. I was glad, for their sake. They were not at all bad, but not near good enough to make a living as bards.

We saw a few other travelers in the main room as more dale folk came in later in the evening. More than I would have expected, actually. The Westernpath road we were on wasn't used very much as the only thing it led to was a village a few days beyond where we encountered Laonid, and some ancient ruins beyond that. The road and path through the forest was created back when the ruined city was alive, but no one recalls how long ago that might have been. Most of the traffic in and out of Daerwoe went by the Northpath road, which lead to Ta Connor, the seat of the Kingdom.

The four of us started talking about various topics, feeling some of the weariness of the trip leave and our muscles relax. It was mostly Jon, Terrin, and I who spoke while Randy listened. He'd occasionally ask a question about something he didn't understand, but he mostly just sat and nodded—though I could tell he found it hard to follow our conversations about whether Chancellor Emil was going to send more soldiers to the Marches, and who was a better 'smith: Derek from here in Boarderdale or Redman from northern Daerwoe. Randy would politely mention something about where he came from, but not arrogantly like he had the day before. It was a nice evening.

At some point I was looking around the main room and noticed a couple travelers looking at us. They spoke a few words to each other, drank, and kept staring. I locked eyes with one of them and kept my face blank. He just looked back, but with a calculating expression. Randy was watching and listening to the players and enjoying their banter with patrons, Terrin was sitting with his eyes closed, and Jon was collecting another bowl of stew from a girl that looked a lot like the innkeeper. "Jon, do you recognize those two guys over there under the window?"

Jon sucked some spilled stew off his hand and looked over. "The guy on the left looks familiar but not the other."

"Last Autumn, at Baker's Mill?"

"Yeah, I think so. He was one of the guys who tried to torch the place."

Terrin opened his eyes and followed our gaze. He wasn't with Jon and me that week when we were hired to protect Baker and his property from threats he had been receiving. We were two of several mercenaries who they hired as guards. The guy we recognized was one of the vandals that had tried to set fire to the mill and house. We stopped them, put out one small fire, and caused only one death and a few serious injuries. If I recall, this guy was unusual. The other vandals were seemingly paid just to start fires, and mostly fled when the danger to them got too high, but this guy seemed to have been there more for the conflict than as arsonist-for-hire. He gave most of the serious wounds to the guards before fleeing on his own. I think I have a scar or two from that encounter.

By now even Randy was looking alternately between them and us. Neither group was making any gestures or expressions to provoke or intimidate the other, but there was still a palpable tension in the air. After a couple minutes the familiar one of the two drained his mug then winked in our direction. The two of them got up together and sauntered out of the inn and into the night. We watched them leave and kept our eyes on the closed door. When a young couple walked in we broke our gazes and turned to each other.

"What do you think?" Terrin began.

Jon replied, only *half* joking I presume, "Perhaps we should sleep with water buckets beside our beds."

"I'd never met the torcher before The Mill and not since, until now. We can't just assume he's up to no good. It's possible he's just traveling through or on some innocent errand," I tried.

Terrin and Randy watched Jon and me as we spoke. "No, I have a feeling he's back in town for a reason. I don't believe he's from Daerwoe unless he's far underground. And if he is, it's certain he's up to no good," Jon said between bites of nearly forgotten stew.

Randy looked half curious and concerned, but didn't speak.

Terrin asked, "Do you think he recognized you and might think we're a threat to whatever he's doing here?"

We considered. "I don't know. He recognized us as we did him, but as for what he thinks of us I have no clue." I looked back to the door, "But I'll volunteer to take first watch."

We fell silent for some time after that. The music and the good spirits of the growing patrons only helped to take the darkness from our thoughts, but not the lingering concerns themselves. After a while, we agreed it was time to turn in, and leave as early as we could the next morning.

We had a room large enough for the four of us to spread out comfortably. There were two wood-framed rope beds and many spare blankets. Terrin and Randy got the beds, and I set up near the door. As the night got older I heard my companions' breathing change from restless to slumber one by one.

* * * *

The next morning came without incident. We all awoke early from being well rested rather than waking up early because of the usual hard, cold ground. Sleep, the sun, the sounds of people outside on their way to the fields or their shops, all conspired to put us into another good mood.

Randy was singing a medley of songs from his homeland, and while I hadn't heard them before, I'm pretty sure they were not all intended to be off key. But I found it enjoyable just the same. If everything went well he'd likely be back home before the day was gone. In the common room, over a breakfast of potato, onion, delicious lamb, and even some apple cobbler, he'd expressed how excited he was to be going back. He said it would be nice to spend some time here, but only if it were a lot more safe and he knew for sure he'd be able to go back. When he said that, I could tell he was hiding some worry about today. I'd told him, not wanting to ruin his high spirits but also not wanting him to be as devastated as he could become if it didn't work out, that while it's extremely likely all would go well, we weren't completely certain. He appeared to view that with healthy realism. I hoped.

We set off just as the sun appeared above the hills in the direction we were going. It was going to be a warm day, but as we rode out of the village as the dew still blanketed everything and the shadows from the hills reached far across the plain. Our horses seemed glad to have had a night under shelter and given fresh oats; they appeared cheerful as well.

We'd pretty much forgotten the events of the previous night until Jon reigned to a stop and whistled through his teeth in alarm only seconds before five horsemen rode into view down the road. They came toward us at a leisurely pace, and I could see the two from last night were among them. Yet the torcher was not their leader. The man in front was a rather large and muscular fellow with a longsword on his back. He had a long moustache and beard and wore his sandy hair in an impressive braid. He had the look of a Northerner; unusual considering the other four men were obviously from the Middlelands.

When he was within several yards from us he signaled his group to stop. "Alright, let's not quibble. We're here for the Wizard's body. Give it to us and we'll let you go. There's no need for unnecessary bloodshed."

I spoke for our group, saying, "What right do you have over our bounty?"

"It's not the bounty we're after, but rather the body itself. Don't waste time—I'm not a very patient man. Release it now or we take it."

I couldn't imagine what he'd want the body for except to present to the Wizard's Council themselves; but, regardless, we weren't going to just hand it over. I looked over at Jon, who rose an eyebrow to indicate he was willing and able. Terrin rode forward between Jon and me to make a barrier between this group and the mule, which still carried both litter and Randy. We were all agreed. Well, the three of us. I could only guess what Randy was thinking.

"Sir, we do not recognize your claim, and refuse to hand over what is rightfully ours. Stand aside and let us pass." I could hardly hear myself through the blood rushing through my ears. My muscles tightened, my spine tingled, my guts knotted.

I wasn't surprised when he drew his monstrous sword, cueing the rest of his group to follow suit, and yelled, "Then we'll take your lives as well!" and charged. The two riders next to the Northerner charged with him while the remaining two stayed back. The road was too narrow to allow them to enter the fight directly.

Jon took the blow from the big man's longsword, blocking it with his own blade. The sound was deafening. The

Northerner charged on past. The other two stopped on either side of Terrin and me, swinging their broadswords. I blocked and swung, was blocked and blocked again. My arm felt like water after each block only to become rigid again in time to make an attack of my own.

I saw Terrin back his horse up to get closer to Randy, rebuffing his attacker at the same time. My opponent and I circled the ground on our horses as we exchanged blows until my back was to the other two riders. Just as I realized my exposure, I heard the charge of a horse behind me. I broke off from my opponent and trotted forward toward Jon who had turned and closed in again with the Northerner several trots behind Randy and the mule. I passed Terrin to come up beside Randy before I turned back toward the front of the battle.

My first opponent, and the guy who had been sitting with the torcher the previous night, were right on me but at least I was in a better position. One fighter had to pass me on my left swinging with his far arm. He missed wildly and kept going while the second one pulled his mount to a stop directly in front of me. Neither of us were able to do anything to the other from this distance, but Terrin was only a sidestep from reaching him for me. Just as the attacker moved to charge on my right, between Randy and me, Terrin swung back, hard, to wedge his sword deep into the man's side. He then charged forward, weaponless, past his own challenger.

The wounded man's horse continued to carry him, screaming, past me where I was able to grab Terrin's sword and wrench it out of his torso which pulled him to the ground in the process. Terrin turned back sharply and charged forward, pulling two knives from under his vest. He yelled and scowled as he closed in with his original attacker. He'd moved in fast enough to duck in under the man's swing and throw himself into the other, both falling to the ground.

I turned my horse in time to see the torcher's friend also turning back toward me. Behind him was Jon and the

Northerner circling and making short charges past each other. My opponent and I closed in with our own short charge and locked blades side-by-side. I had Terrin's blade in my right hand keeping the enemy's blade locked between blade and pommel while I swung my own sword with my other arm. He couldn't force his sword free in time to defend, so he took the blade in his raised defending arm. It was a bad swing and glanced off his forearm bracer and cut shallowly into his shoulder. I tried to swing back again but it was an even worse swing and he caught it in his gloved hand. I tried to push the sword forward to cut through the leather, but he just went with it. He dropped his own sword and with his free hand punched me in the face. I was more surprised than wounded, but that allowed him the chance to let go of my sword and use both hands to grab my throat. He was in too close, much too close for me to use either sword with any effectiveness. I dropped both blades, brought my arms in and tried to hit his forearms up from the bottom, but that just succeeded in hurting me more. My vision got fuzzy and the pain in my chest was getting worse. I could vaguely feel the horses stepping and moving under us.

I did the only thing I could think of doing: I grabbed the saddle and pushed away as hard as I could. I fell over backward and onto the ground on my rear. Sparks shot through my back and stars in my eyes, but I could breathe deep, ragged breaths. The attacker, unbalanced by my move, had also fallen. He wasn't as bad off as I was because he got back up and came toward me with one of the dropped swords in hand. I couldn't get up; my legs didn't want to respond. I pulled my dagger but knew I couldn't do anything to protect myself from a powerful overhand blow from a sword. I raised it, hoping I might get lucky and able to deflect the first blow enough to live long enough to do some damage, when I saw movement from the side.

Randy had the sword Jon gave him days before and swung it wildly into the attacker's back. The man's eyes went wide and he gasped silently. His legs crumpled useless below him, putting him on my level. I had to strike quick and sure: I lunged from the ground and plunged my dagger into his chest just below the breastbone, and up, twisted. The sword fell out of his hands and his gaze melted far away. His body fell to the side.

I looked up and saw Randy standing, looking both morose and agitated down at the body. I looked around, ready for another attack. I saw the Northerner riding down the road away from Jon who was now standing on the ground. To my right was Terrin examining the body with the gash in its side. His other attacker was lying nearby with knives in either side of his neck. Down the road was the torcher, still on his horse, having watched it all. He smiled at me and winked before kicking his horse into a gallop to follow the Northerner. Jon watched the guy come his direction, moving out of sword range. The torcher just rode on past and down the road out of sight.

I got up and was at least able to stand, if shakily, as the numbness left my legs. I looked at Randy, and he looked back at me. He was still breathing heavily and unconsciously rubbing his hands on his pants. He looked like he wanted to say something but wasn't sure what to say. He turned and walked a little down the road. Jon passed him on his way to me and watched for a few steps over his shoulder.

"Are you hurt?" Jon asked me.

I evaluated myself. My back was enflamed, but was fading with each moment into a stabbing ache. My throat still hurt, but all in all I was fine. I told him so. He had a cut over his right eye, but was also basically unhurt. "My arms feel as brittle as a clay pot; that was one of the best swordfights I've had in a long time. He was certainty an experienced fighter."

Terrin joined us. He had a bad bruise on his cheek, and his cut from a couple days ago was seeping again. He could certainly use a few days of quiet. "Why? Who are they and why did they want Laonid?" We all looked over at the body, safe and sound, on the litter behind the mule. I looked back at Randy. He was standing in the road looking up at the sky.

"Well, let's collect what's ours. We can inform the gate guards at Daerwoe what happened here. C'mon."

* * * *

By the time Randy joined us in the sitting room, the sun had set and the plates of meats, cheeses, and vegetables had been picked over pretty well. Terrin stood at the tall window looking out over the city. His cheek was still swollen, but the Stone's chiurgen closed and tended the cut well. Jon sat in one of the biggest chairs I'd ever seen and gazed into the swirling wine in his goblet. I sat nearby in thought. Scribe Havlin explained to us how certain individuals could want Laonid's body in order to sell it to other certain Necromancers who would use it to gain more power and essence—which explained the Northerner and his fellow mercenaries. The Scribe had also given us our payment for services rendered, which made me feel unusually uncomfortable about the whole "mercenary" label.

Randy was led back into the room by a robed aide and looked tired and thoughtful. He sat down on the couch next to me and sighed. "Well, it's not one hundred percent, but they think it's likely all will work out OK. They did some hocus-pocus stuff on me, said the planets are still aligned just right, or something, to let it be possible—but only by tonight."

The aide handed Randy a goblet of wine. Randy thanked him, drank, looked into the goblet like he expected to see something, then drank again. "The thing is, I can accept people from my . . . planet, getting zapped over here. People go missing every day. But, well, people don't reappear saying they came from some fantasy land. Unless they're crazy or want to get into a tabloid. So, I'm wondering just how likely it will work. What if . . . what if something goes horribly wrong and I'm beamed into a volcano or something."

Jon asked, "Thinking of staying here?" Since the encounter in the hills, Jon started showing Randy more deference and friendliness. To Jon, Randy showed bravery and courage earlier in the day. That may be, but I could see Randy was still bothered and would probably remain so for quite some time. He came from a place where people could be expected to live their entire lives having never experienced violence, and would soon be going back there. While here, he commits something that in his own land, society, upbringing, would be seen as brutal barbarism.

"No, I have to take the chance, don't I? I don't belong here. Even if the odds are against me, and the wizards end up sending me into deep space or something, I have to take the chance. I have a home and a life back there, and if I can't go back to that, it's not worth being anywhere else." We were all silent for a while, each with our own thoughts.

Finally, the aide announced that it was time for Randy to go, the Council was ready for him. We all stood, and as if the silence had gotten so heavy it broke, Jon started to chuckle. Terrin smiled and sighed as if letting out a held breath, and Randy and I finally smiled. "Well, so this is it. I hope you had a nice vacation." He laughed.

Jon grasped Randy's forearm with one hand and his shoulder with the other. "Go with a new heart."

"Yeah, I will." He smiled at Jon and nodded.

Terrin grasped Randy's arm and said, "We're glad you came around. I think you saved one or more of our lives once, maybe twice. You're good luck."

"Well, . . ." he tried, blushing.

"Oh," Terrin continued, rummaging in his cloak. "Here, you can have this back." He handed Randy his little black phone. Randy blushed harder and tucked it away stammering. Terrin cut him off, laughing, "Go in health."

Randy nodded and turned to me. I placed my hands on his shoulders and smiled. "Thank you. For . . . many things." He looked at me quizzically but pleased. "Go, return home.

Get back to your life, and don't forget to live it."

"Thanks. I certainly won't forget *this* as long as I live."

He turned to the aide holding the door open for him. "Well, guys, uhm, take care. It was an adventure." He backed up to the door then held up his hand as he walked out. Terrin and I held up ours until he was gone and the aide closed the door behind them.

Jon turned around to collect his wine. "That's that. Given some time he could have made a good companion."

"Right now I'm just thinking of a soft bed and a fire and some sleep." Terrin picked up his sword belt and got set to head to our guest apartments.

I reached into my trouser pocket and pulled out the card I had gotten from my pack before they took our things to our rooms. It was in a pouch, in a box, at the bottom of the pack. I literally hadn't looked at it in years, and it felt so alien in my hand. I'm not sure why I retrieved it that night, or why I had even kept it in the first place. But it probably had something to do with those feelings I let go into the creek the other night. Feelings that still lingered and cried out to me to sort out.

I was afraid, though. Afraid that if I embraced those feelings and memories, it would prevent me from living my life here as they had once done. Or, was I now better prepared to deal with them?

I turned the smooth card over and looked at myself in it— a younger, more innocent self. Along the top were words that looked both unusual and familiar: "Driver's License, State of Iowa," and below that were little bits of information about a sixteen-year-old Sarah. A Sarah that went missing from her home only days after proudly earning that little card.

"Are you coming?" Terrin asked, half out the door.

I put the card back into my pocket, brushed a lock of hair behind my ear, and followed my companions back out into the life I am living.

SINGULARITY DEFERRED:
CHAPTER ONE

I wrote and re-wrote the following chapter to my novel more times than I can count. I started writing it, like "The Sword Remembers," back in the halcyon undergrad days—but unlike that effort, this one didn't come alive; it didn't speak to me. It was always work when I plucked away at it. Yet, I couldn't let it go and about once a year I would bring it back up and work on it, re-writing it again, sometimes going on to a second chapter that would be deleted come the next time I gave it another go. Unlike countless other story and novel attempts that have rightfully been conceded into oblivion, this one nagged at me to live. "For Whom the Tinker Toils" dared me to bring it to life, but was playful and supportive in its obstinate struggle. "The Sword Remembers" required effort, but like the sculptor, the work was in removing the debris that covered a story that was eager to be free. Singularity Deferred resisted my efforts, and I resent it for that. Until, that is, I finally met the grad school professor that would become my mentor. He gave me inspiration and focus, not just as a writer, but as a human being—and like the mystical monk who will not come to teach until the student is ready, this novel finally let me in and showed me what it wanted to be. I wrote this chapter in minutes, then the next chapter . . . and after nearly a decade of work in writing the first chapter, the entire 110,000-word novel was written in sixteen months.

I woke up to what sounded like fireworks going off in a coffee can, and I was in that can. A sound that was less a *sound* than a full-body reverberation. I felt it through the hard metal floor and in my bones. As much as my body kept trying to keep me down, convincing me I needed to keep sleeping, I fought the fog and climbed into that kind of wakefulness where you can't quite clear your head and get a grip of where you are and what's going on around you–made all the worse in this case by the fact I *didn't* know where I was.

Wherever I was, the room was dimly lit by weak and sputtering fluorescent lights hinting at metal walls, floor, low ceiling; smooth, dirty-white crates and bins here and there; and at my feet some unusual piece of machinery that reminded me of three interlocked bicycle tires stuck in the middle of a pile of computer parts. Lying against it was my mother's long, heavy, silver flashlight. *What the heck was that doing there?* I thought. *Forget that, what am I doing here?* I sat up, trying to remember anything about what led up to this moment.

Another felt-not-heard explosion caught my attention, and I struggled to my feet. Then struggled to my feet again. I felt unbelievably weak, unbalanced, like right after a too long, too hard weight lifting session (which, as anyone could tell by looking at the hundred and fifty pound me, I did not commit often), and it took a few tries to stagger to the door until I collapsed against the wall. I felt both concerned by my unusual condition and a little disgusted by my physical state, as if I had suffered through a nasty bout of flu, wearing the same clothes the whole time.

I pushed a recessed, oblong "open" button next to the door which slid aside into the wall, revealing a short, narrow corridor that reminded me of movie submarines: exposed wiring ducts and odd pieces of metal frame jutting here and there. All of it painted a dull white. I called out, "Hello?" No response. Narrow doors to the front, left and right. I called out again, and again no one responded. I struggled against the wall, making unintentionally wild steps and over-reaching for portions of the bulkhead, unable to find my balance or completely control my limbs.

Once I got to the door in front, I peered through the little smoked-glass window set at eye level. Inside looked like the cockpit of a plane, and my confusion started to solidify into a needling anxiety. *How in the world did I get into a plane? What in the world did I do last night? Why is there no one in the cockpit?*

I pushed the open button for this door and a loud, rhythmic beeping flooded out. I examined the three windows in front. Black. Very black. I figured it was the darkest night I'd ever seen, or something was covering the glass. The cockpit was tight and cramped–I had to literally climb into the single large, black chair. I looked over my shoulder out the door to see if anyone had come yet (no one had), then turned my attention to the console of . . . controls that didn't look like any airplane controls I was familiar with. Instead of toggles and dials and a yoke, the console was covered with all manner of computer screens and small clusters of buttons. Some of the smaller monitors showed images I couldn't make out: circles, lines and curves, scrolling numbers and words. Some looked like animated navigational charts, in full color 3-D even, while others looked like calculators gone insane. One of the main monitors in front caught my eye:

–HULL DAMAGE: undetectable. (.0045 stress factor)
Course deviation corrected – minimal energy usage
–COMMUNICATIONS HAIL (23.2.88)
–COMMUNICATIONS HAIL (23.5.40)
–Incoming object (q67754)
—SRS Identification: energy based (factor 7)
–NEAR PROXIMITY ENERGY RELEASE–
—Gauss Barriers inactive -4-
–HULL DAMAGE: undetectable (.016 stress factor)

–Unidentified Craft: distance at 66k (5-5-7)
Course deviation corrected – minimal energy usage
–COMMUNICATIONS HAIL (23.16.82)
The last line appeared as I read, causing the first line to scroll off the top of the screen. If this was what was currently going on, I assumed someone was trying to call us. I craned back around and yelled again, "Hello? Anyone out there?" and again received no reply. I looked around the console at buttons and words that were just too many to take in. A small monitor off to my right had one flashing label on its face, in a couple of rows of touch-screen icons. The flashing one read "Communications." *Why not*, I thought.

I touched it and the other icons disappeared with a set of new virtual buttons replacing them. I could make sense of most of them. I did what seemed most obvious and pressed "receive Xmission." Instantly, the loud beeping turned into a slight background noise and, while the control screen I was paying attention to didn't change, the main one in the middle showed some movement. Turning my attention to it, I was surprised but relieved to see a person looking back at me. A man of some exotic ethnic decent I couldn't place. No hair on head nor face, angular structure, dark complexion.

"How good of you to answer," he said in a gravelly baritone. "It took some work getting your attention." Actually, what he *really* said was something like: "*Masayang proper tú comeback la sig-wei. Nulij'yu tú ears up.*" I never got proficient at speaking the mix-up of Spanish, English, and various Asian languages that formed the predominant tongue spoken by most traders, haulers, pirates, and the like, but I eventually got good at understanding it. Not at that point I wasn't, though.

"Uh, I'm sorry I have no idea what you just said." He looked right at me through the screen, examining me as I was him. I glanced up and around quickly for the lens of a camera but saw none.

He continued, but in a simplistic English still peppered

with slang I had to guess at. The conversation went more or less like: "Who are you? You're not Jarrod. You do look a lot like him. . . . Where is he?"

"I, uh" I began most eloquently, "I don't know any 'Jarrod'. In fact, to be perfectly honest, I don't even know where I am. Could–"

"Humorous," he interrupted, "We detected only one person on board, so either he's dead, or you've taken his ship, or both." He had a creepy smile: "As much as I would appreciate that, I'm going to guess it's more likely he's run off, as expected, and you're covering for him." (That last bit, he actually said the figure of speech, "*y tú fuzzfacin' dachi.*" I could never hear that and keep a straight face. I had to constantly have him rephrase what he said, which certainly contributed to his bad attitude.)

"Look, I'm sorry, I really am, but I'm in some trouble here. I honestly don't know how I got here–I woke up, and here I was. No one else seems to be here, and I'd really like to know where I am and why."

He continued as if I hadn't spoken, "To come to the point, Jarrod, you, both of you, I don't care, there's something of mine Jarrod took from me, and I intend to get it back. I'm willing, for old times' sake, to ask nicely and forget this happened. Maybe. But the more I'm delayed, the more apt I am to simply take it back. At whatever cost, to whoever has it."

"Okay, go ahead. Seriously. Come aboard and get it, whatever it is, and then tell me how to get back down or up or, uh . . . over, or what-the-heck-ever. Better yet, take me with you, and we can find Jarrod together and get some answers. I like that one, actually."

He snorted, "Funny. We already know it's not on your ship. If you really don't know what you're doing there, I'd say that's *your* problem. Since neither Jarrod nor my property is currently on board, I'm going to give him one chance. And you give him this message: He's to meet me on Sandiki in ten seds. If he doesn't, I won't come politely knocking next time. Understand?"

"Hey, I–"

"Hao." The monitor clicked to darkness, followed after a pause by:

–Communication terminated (23.42.7)

–Ship Identified – NT: *Tsaul Ki* (revenant class)

–*Tsaul Ki* distance +5.33k -> (5-5-7 . . . . . . 5-8-7+)

I sat in silence, uncertain what exactly just happened. Who was that? What in the heck was that all about? The only thing that came to mind was *I'm back where I began*. Except, now I had some communication controls, at least. I felt a little more collected despite my situation, what with having some human contact–even if weird and belligerent.

I turned my attention back to the little monitor on the right for clues as to how to reach anyone else on it. Some of the labels on buttons and panel sections on the console started to catch my attention. At first, I couldn't quite make sense of the words, as if the odd lettering made the word unreadable, then I realized I was reading things I simply couldn't have expected to see: "Shield control," "astrogation," "artfl. gravity control. . . ."

I started looking around more closely, reading everything, becoming increasingly curious, then disbelieving, then nervous. "Orbit modulation," "anti-matter drive control," "dark-matter focal control," and finally my eyes happened upon and stopped at "fore-window opacity." That set had an oblong button with "+" and "-" symbols on either end. I looked up at the three blackened windows in front of me, separated by thin strips of hull structure just barely keeping the triptych of glass from being one long swath of ebony. Without looking away from the middle window, I depressed the "-" end of the flat button and watched as the dull black steadily dissipated to allow what was outside become visible, like window tinting fading away. What came into view was a similar yet deeper blackness filled with pinpoints of light. Just to the right and below, the size of an orange held at arm's length, was the most beautiful and terrifying image of what could be nothing other than an alien planet. Not the blue of Neptune or Uranus, or the orange-striped Jupiter, ringed Saturn, red Mars, or blue and white Earth–but something I'd never seen in any astronomy text or television program. It was a disk of green, brown, and yellow stripes slowly but visibly grinding against each other as they moved across the surface, causing little eddies of storms at the meeting places.

A planet. Stars and a planet not just out and forward, or above, but *below* my eye-level, where if I were in a plane I should have been able to see land. I felt dizzy and nauseated, weak and light-headed. I put my head between my knees for a few minutes and controlled my breathing. It was a while before I could convince myself to look back up.

ABOUT THE AUTHOR

Liam was born and raised primarily in Colorado, in the shadows of the Rocky Mountains, then lost for a while in the midwest. He currently lives in Oregon with his wife and daughter and too many books crying from the shelves, demanding to be read. He has a Masters Degree in English with a focus on creative writing (yes, come to find out, such a thing actually *is* possible) and plans to continue on to an MFA or PhD. In the meantime, he has completed his first full-length science fiction novel, *Singularity Deferred*, and is in the process of finding appropriate hiking boots.

Connect online:
Website and blog: www.tragic-sans.com
Facebook: www.facebook.com/LiamRWDoyle
Twitter: twitter.com/tragicsans